GHOSTS OF
BLUEWATER CREEK

The one thing on the mind of man hunter Josh McCabe is to bring in Abe Lawton: the last and most vicious member of a gang who killed his wife and son. Now that time has arrived, but Josh doesn't count on a smart-mouthed kid out for revenge and a girl in the wrong place at the wrong time. The showdown comes quickly — but it's far from decisive and leaves all three facing a new, more dangerous future.

Books by Terry James
in the Linford Western Library:

LONG SHADOWS
ECHOES OF A DEAD MAN

TERRY JAMES

GHOSTS OF BLUEWATER CREEK

Complete and Unabridged

LINFORD
Leicester

First published in Great Britain in 2011 by
Robert Hale Limited
London

First Linford Edition
published 2013
by arrangement with
Robert Hale Limited
London

British Library CIP Data

James, Terry.
  Ghosts of Bluewater Creek. - -
  (Linford western library)
  1. Western stories.
  2. Large type books.
  I. Title II. Series
  823.9'2–dc23

  ISBN 978–1–4448–1490–3

Published by
F. A. Thorpe (Publishing)
Anstey, Leicestershire

Set by Words & Graphics Ltd.
Anstey, Leicestershire
Printed and bound in Great Britain by
T. J. International Ltd., Padstow, Cornwall

This book is printed on acid-free paper

1

Josh McCabe pushed open the door of the sheriff's office and dropped the burden from his shoulder. It made a dead, heavy sound as it hit the rough boards and around the room everything from the glass in the windows to the gun rack on the wall rattled. Only the sheriff, a big, sweat-stained man with a long moustache and a flabby paunch seemed undisturbed by the commotion. If it hadn't been for the gentle rustle of the newspaper as he turned to the next page, a casual observer might have thought the man with his feet up on the desk was asleep on the job.

But Josh didn't underestimate anyone.

'Sorry,' he said, closing the door gently before helping himself to a cup of hot coffee from a pot on the stove.

With a sigh, the sheriff finally looked up. Removing his glasses, he folded the wire arms flat before slipping them into his shirt pocket. Then he kicked his feet to the ground and peered over his desk at the body on the floor before giving Josh a full head-to-toe once over.

'I could probably arrest you for that,' he said, without a hint of humour.

Josh chuckled and tossed a folded piece of paper on to the lawman's desk. 'John Travis. The dodger says dead or alive. I thought I'd save you some time and the town the expense of keeping him while you wait for a judge to come through and hang him.'

The sheriff grunted, digging a toe into the corpse as he passed to refill his coffee cup. 'I was talking about you making a goddamn mess on my floor.'

Josh nodded, his initial good humour fading under the sheriff's continuing lack of interest. 'Of course you were. The poster says five hundred dollars. I'm in a hurry. Have you got the money in the safe?'

'Five hundred?'

'It says it there in black and white.'

Josh pointed to the untouched dodger.

'What did he do, steal candy from a five year old?'

The sheriff's contempt continued to erode Josh's temper. 'He killed his family, then rode into town spraying bullets and killed another five people before high-tailing it with the banker's daughter,' he reported without emotion.

They stood a moment or two in silence while the sheriff inspected the wanted poster and Josh stared at the corpse. He had been a boy, only sixteen, the peach fuzz on his chin confirming his tender years. Even with the cuts and bruises Josh's fists had inflicted, in death his face took on an angelic innocence that belied the evil inside.

'Did you find the girl?'

'Nope. I don't think I would have wanted to.'

The sheriff seemed curious as he glanced sideways and narrowed his eyes at Josh, but if he had intended to probe further, something changed his mind and Josh was glad of it. If Travis's dying confession was true . . .

Josh's anger flared as he wished he could kill the twisted son-of-a-bitch again.

The stove hissed as he tossed the dregs of his cup into its belly. 'About that reward money . . . '

The sheriff pursed his lips and inflated his chest, working up to something. Josh had a pretty good idea what. He had been stonewalled more than once by a lawman who didn't like bounty hunters and resented paying out more than his own yearly wage to someone he considered no more than a saddle tramp with a gun.

Before he could attempt a refusal, Josh pointed to a wanted poster pinned to the notice board behind the sheriff's desk. 'I heard a rumour Abe Lawton's headed this way. Some bummer saw him in Bluewater a couple of weeks ago. The guy said he was tearing down the town: drinking, beating and killing men, raping women.'

'Bluewater? That's less than fifty miles away from here. Do you reckon he's headed this way?'

'He could be.'

'Is that why you're in a hurry to get out of town?' The sheriff's comment dripped with scorn.

'I was more thinking about you. I wouldn't want to get in your way when you make your play.'

The sheriff's jowls wobbled as he gulped. He obviously hadn't thought about his own involvement, and now Josh mentioned it he didn't like the prospect.

'Do you fancy your chances trying to bring him in?' the lawman asked, sounding more desperate than conversational.

'I always like to finish a job when I start it.'

Josh's remark made the sheriff turn and scrutinize him, his brow furrowing before his eyes widened. The news seemed to light a fuse under the apathetic sheriff and he rattled the keys on his belt as he almost tripped over the corpse in his haste to get to the safe. His fingers fairly shook as he pulled out a stack of bills and counted off $500 into Josh's rock-steady hand.

'You're him, aren't you?' he said, shoving the remainder into the safe and locking the door. He handed Josh a receipt slip, waited for him to sign it using a pen from the desk, then stared at the neat signature. 'I knew I was right. You're that bounty hunter who brought in the other four Lawtons. Well, Mr McCabe, I can't say I like what your kind does, but you . . . you've got my respect for that at least.'

Josh headed for the door, barely able to contain a smirk of satisfaction. True he'd been trying to put the fear of God — or the Devil — into the sheriff, but it didn't hurt to have smoke blown up your ass now and again. It beat the alternative. But he didn't have time for chitchat and definitely couldn't force himself to trade empty niceties with an

6

official who had probably been elected by default and would probably look the other way if trouble did make an appearance in his town. Besides, if Abe Lawton was near by, Josh didn't want to miss the son-of-a-bitch again.

'I'm keeping his horse,' Josh said, nodding towards Travis. 'Have you got a problem with that, Sheriff?'

'No, sir, anything that takes you closer to keeping Abe Lawton away from this town is fine by me. Do you think you'll be able to? Stop him before he gets here, I mean.'

Josh grunted, leaving the lazy old man in no doubt about his disdain for him. Looking somewhat put out, but now too nervous even for caustic sarcasm, the lawman shook his head as he pulled out his spectacles and returned to his desk. 'On your way to the livery stables, ask the undertaker to come over and collect this body, will you?'

Josh stepped outside, bracing himself against an onslaught of lashing rain.

Deliberately, he left the door open, noting the puddle that quickly spread inside. 'Ask him yourself,' he called over his shoulder as he collected the horses from the hitch rail before heading back along the street.

2

Standing in the middle of nowhere, Ellen Cahill shifted her old carpetbag from her left hand to her right and back again, trying to ease the stiffness in her arms. It didn't help. Her back still ached, her feet hurt and her head pounded like a blacksmith's hammer.

She had imagined that losing her money, her ticket and being thrown off a train was the worst that could happen, not counting what she still couldn't think about in Bluewater. Now, cold and tired with three-day-old hunger gnawing at her backbone, she admitted she was probably wrong. She had been walking for two days and the only sign of civilization she had seen was an old boot with a hole in the sole half-buried at the side of the road.

She looked up at the sky, swaying slightly as the movement caused a sudden wave of dizziness to wash over her. Determined not to faint again, she drew in a deep breath, then let it out slowly as she waited for the sensation to pass and her vision to clear. Overhead, the encroaching black clouds only added to her feeling of desolation as they shadowed the lush green valley and slowly turned day as dark as night. Even the distant mountains lost their silvery brilliance as the heavens dropped a veil over their snow-capped peaks.

Returning her attention to the road, Ellen blinked rapidly against tears of despair she thought had long since dried up. 'Oh, stop it,' she said, dabbing her eyes on a torn cuff. 'What other choice do you have?'

Looking down at her plain black dress, she frowned as she realized that even it had seen better days. Like her courage it too was falling apart at the seams in the face of a harsh reality. A splash of rain hit her in the face. Another. Then another. That was all she needed, and she said as much as she rolled her eyes and scowled at the sky.

She grabbed up her skirts with fresh determination and started to walk the road that seemed without end as her rain-soaked dress weighted down every step. Stumbling for what seemed like the hundredth time, she allowed herself to cry at last as mud and blood trickled down her shins. But her tears weren't formed from self-pity. They were a bitter mix of disappointment and defeat, because, despite her bravado back in Bluewater, she had failed in her quest at the first obstacle.

But no, she couldn't allow herself to fail.

'Get up, girl,' she told herself as she fell again. 'Get up!'

Somehow she scrambled to her feet and managed another step, but fatigue and the growing certainty that she was destined to die in this miserable, god-forsaken place weighed like rocks in her boots. This time when she fell she stayed face down in the mud, feeling it suck her in like an old friend's embrace as the rain patted her on the back, congratulating her on a decision well made.

She thought again about the boot, separated from its partner and left half-buried and forgotten beside the road. Would the folks who found her cold, dead body just walk on by as she had done? Or would they wonder who she was, where she came from or what madness had brought a sixteen-year-old girl to this remote place?

The cruel facts acted like a slap in the face.

'I want to live,' she muttered, somehow pushing herself on to her hands, then her knees and finally to her feet. 'I have to live.'

The world reeled, flashing silver and black before her eyes, but now she didn't let it stop her as she repeated the words, using them like a crutch as she forced one foot in front of the other, again and again.

When at last a town appeared up

ahead she was long past believing in a happy ending. Without really trusting her eyes, she stumbled down the middle of the main street looking in awe at the people who, in turn, stopped to stare at her.

Like a desert oasis, a beautiful hotel loomed before her with its brightly painted sign shining through the greyness of the day. Remembering her appearance, she stopped and tried to run her fingers through her sodden, knotted hair then she straightened her collar and sleeves.

'Get out of the road,' a rider shouted, mud splashing her as a horse walked past.

She leapt out of the way, missing her footing in a deep puddle. The world spun as her arms fanned the air, pain jarring through her as she landed heavily on the rutted ground. Pride made her struggle against the sticky wetness that sought to hold her, but fighting only seemed to make the situation worse. Already drenched, lightheaded from lack of food and sore from a dozen falls, the last of her strength ebbed away quickly with her fruitless efforts.

She stopped fighting. This time she wasn't worried. It didn't matter. She lay back and waited, allowing the dizziness and constant pounding in her head to engulf her as she imagined a plate of food, a clean bed and the safe embrace of a woman she only knew as a pretty face in a faded tintype.

3

'What's she doing?' a man on the street shouted.

Fresh from stabling the horses, Josh was heading for the saloon. He didn't miss a stride as he negotiated a bunch of folks too stupid to get out of the rain. Small towns were full of crazy people and he had learned not to stick his nose in where it didn't belong. Besides, his mouth tasted like an old washrag, his stomach growled and nothing and no one was standing in the way of a bottle of whiskey and a plate of mutton and potatoes. Even so, he couldn't shake a feeling of foreboding as the crack of a whip and the creak of wheels warned him the stage was on its way.

He pulled away as someone grabbed his arm, losing his footing on the uneven plankwalk and glaring at the elderly woman who yanked him to the front of the crowd. 'Can't you help her, big man?'

Without thinking, he let his gaze follow the direction of the woman's outstretched finger. It was difficult to make out the figure lying in the middle of the street, covered as it was in mud, but he assumed it to be a girl or a woman; a damn fool female at any rate.

Looking along the street, he sighted six angry horses fighting the bit, their powerful hoofs carving out safe passage for the stage. The driver shouted at them, hunkering down inside his coat until his face almost disappeared under his wide brimmed hat.

A sick feeling crept over Josh as he looked quickly between the unshifting crowd, the girl and the vehicle heading towards them. He stepped off the plankwalk, or the old woman pushed him, he wasn't sure which, but his boots slipped and sank as he left the relative safety of the boards. A hush descended over the bystanders as they waited for him to do something.

'Goddamn, useless farmers,' he mumbled under his breath. 'Hey, girly, you better get out of the way.'

Like a deer suddenly aware of the hunter, her head whipped up to find him, her eyes misty and unfocused as she squinted through the relentless downpour. She looked confused, dazed and definitely unaware of the danger bearing down on her.

'Get out of the street,' he yelled.

Her head turned, her expression remaining calm as the stage gathered pace towards her. At last the driver seemed to see her but instead of hauling on the reins he just hollered for her to get out of the way.

Driven forward by the hands of the crowd, Josh slipped and slid his way into the river of mud, his footing precarious as he fought deep ruts and holes caused over time by a hundred wagons and a thousand cattle. Doubting he would make it, he flailed his arms, yelling for her to get back, but she didn't and the horses kept coming.

In his imagination, he could hear them snorting, see their nostrils flare as they fought the driver. Crazy bastard, he was whipping them on!

Gathering momentum as his legs grew accustomed to the sucking mud, Josh snatched the girl up and careered across the street into a sea of boots and skirts as the wheels of the stage churned within inches of his feet.

'Damn fools. Stay out of the street,' the driver yelled.

Someone tried to help Josh up, but he shrugged them off as he rolled his weight off the girl. Lying on her back with her face only inches from his, she blinked rapidly.

'Didn't you see the stage coming?' he asked snappily, raking hair off her muddy face and out of her eyes so she could witness the full ugliness of his anger.

'Are you an angel?' she muttered.

That took the wind out of him. 'Hell no.'

'What did she say?' someone asked.

'Can you walk?' Josh asked, noticing the blood on her knees and shins before he tugged her dress down over her high-buttoned boots.

Her chin trembled.

'Je-sus.' He swept her up and staggered to his feet, glaring at the faces that stared back at him. This was bad. He couldn't afford to be saddled with a girl *or* a reputation as some kind of hero.

'What the hell are you all looking at?' he shouted. 'When I find out who pushed me into the goddamn street . . . '

His harshness had the desired effect with the crowd opening up a path to the hotel. Josh hesitated before taking it. What the hell was he going to do when he got there? In the eyes of the town, he was a man-hunter, outside the boundaries of human decency. He was someone to be feared, if not grudgingly respected when word got round who he was. If he dropped that façade for even a minute . . . and yet, he couldn't just abandon the girl, even if she was a piece of pie short of a picnic. He chuckled to himself. How long had it been since he'd had a simple thought like that?

The girl wrapped her arms around his neck, laying her head against his shoulder. Despite her apparent contentment, she shivered and awkwardly he hugged her more tightly, actually liking the way she snuggled into him, unafraid. It made him feel human, a rare luxury he had denied himself for too long.

'Who does this girl belong to?' he asked, scanning the group of bystanders.

A collection of shrugs and mumbling met his enquiry.

'Well?' Josh asked. 'Is someone going to claim her or do I have to put her back in the road?'

The small crowd had been easing in for a better look but they jumped back and started talking among themselves, feigning a loss of interest if they had to get personally involved.

'Thank you, sir, for your kindness,'

the girl said with quiet dignity, her misty gaze now firmly on him, 'but there'll be no need to toss me aside like an old boot.'

'Do . . . like a what?' he asked, even more certain she wasn't right in the head.

'If you'll please put me down . . . '

He didn't need asking twice but he kept his palm pressed against her back, steadying her as she swayed and looked wide-eyed at the sea of faces.

'I need to see the sheriff,' she said to no one in particular. 'Does anyone know where I can find him?'

Curious looks answered her.

'He rode out of town about five minutes ago,' someone spoke up. 'He said he might not be back for a day or two.'

'Then . . . can anyone tell me where to find Eugenia Allbright?'

Again nothing but muttering met her question.

This time Josh felt the girl's disappointment as whatever faith or optimism she had been relying on dwindled.

'Why don't you wait for the sheriff over at the hotel? I'll send a message to the jail telling him where to find you when he gets back.'

A smile lit up her face, revealing her youth and innocence beneath the layer of dirt. 'That would be wonderful. My name's Ellen Cahill.'

'I'll tell him. Now, why don't you rent a room and get yourself cleaned up.'

She looked down at her muddy dress and her chin trembled as she blinked back tears. 'I can't. I lost my money.'

Reaching into his pocket, he pulled out a couple of dollars and slipped them into her hand.

'Oh no, I couldn't . . . I mean . . . we haven't even been introduced, Mr . . . ?'

He hesitated. The less the girl knew about him the better, but she looked likely to burst into tears if he didn't tell her and he didn't want any more of a scene.

'McCabe,' he mumbled. 'Now just

take the goddamn money. Consider it a loan, if you like.' Backing away, he squared his shoulders and shoved a couple of bystanders aside. 'And stay out of the road, if you know what's good for you. I won't be there to save your crazy ass again.'

'Thank you, Mr McCabe. I won't forget what you've done for me,' she called after him. 'And I'll find a way to pay you back.'

4

The rain had chased more men than usual off the streets and into the saloon but Josh had no trouble finding his way to the bar. Although essentially of a slim build with broad shoulders, his height of over six feet made people step aside without even thinking. Unfortunately, his show out in the street seemed to have added an element of curiosity and he was aware of a dozen faces turned in his direction as he passed through. Out of habit, he set his jaw and squared his shoulders, digging in an elbow here and there and turning his lip in a menacing snarl.

The usual stench of spilt whiskey, cheap perfume and sweat hovered overpoweringly in the moist, smoky air. It turned his already unsettled stomach into a tight knot and, after knocking his hat back to hang by its cord around his neck, he snatched hold of the drink that slid along the bar towards him, taking a moment as he leaned against the scarred top to inhale the sweet scent before swallowing the shot in one gulp.

'You look like you needed that, pard,' a familiar voice drawled, its owner coming into view as the whore who had been standing between them was nudged aside and mingled into the crowd.

Josh sucked in another measured breath, steadying himself against instant irritation. Straight away he wished he hadn't as his churning gut rebelled once more against the lingering stench of unwashed bodies, liquor and cheap cigars. Hunching over his top-up, he filled his nostrils with the smell, finishing the drink in a few measured sips that allowed the liquor to slide warmly down his gullet and soothe his insides.

'Zack Lawton,' he said, the words almost sticking in his craw when he eventually acknowledged the man who had cleared a space for him at the bar and provided the first of what Josh intended to be many drinks. 'Fancy seeing you here,' he said with deliberate sarcasm. 'Am I that predictable now that you know where I'm headed before I do?'

Zack's grin didn't give a clear answer and Josh didn't like it. Maybe trailing after Josh for the best part of a year had taught the kid a few things. Heck, they were already talking like old friends . . . or grudging trail partners at least.

'I sure am glad I was here before you. That was quite an entrance you made. I wouldn't have wanted to miss it.'

Josh stiffened his jaw, his right eye twitching as he tensed. 'You saw what happened?'

Zack, a kid not even into his twenties, half Josh's age, nodded like a wise old sage as he took a sip from his beer. 'The whole town probably saw it. I thought you were going soft.'

'I'm surprised you didn't pull your

gun then and there. It might have been the best chance you ever get to take me down.'

Zack's green eyes twinkled with mischief as he rested his gaze steadily on Josh. 'Surely by now you know I'm not the Lawton you need to be worrying about.'

So that was it. Zack was here to meet Abe. Josh had suspected for a couple of months that the kid was using him to find the older Lawton. It didn't make the inevitable showdown any easier to swallow. Taking one Lawton down was going to be hard enough, but two?

'Maybe, maybe not,' he said, shoving his misgivings to one side.

'Aw, don't be like that. I thought after travelling together — kind of — all these months, we were nearly old friends.'

Josh chuckled. 'I can't see that ever happening, especially after I bring Abe in — dead or alive.'

Zack shrugged nonchalantly.

'I guess you're hoping Abe'll show

you how it's done.' Josh eyed the old .38 holstered against the kid's thigh. 'Have you pulled that iron you're wearing on anything but a tin can yet?'

Zack's fixed grin slipped just a fraction, but instead of biting, he held up his hands in mock surrender. 'Some of those cans can be mighty ornery, you know, but we're not talking about me. What's next for you after that little stunt you just pulled?' He turned to rest his elbows on the bar, burying his chin in the red bandanna about his neck as he tried to stifle a laugh. 'Rescuing stray dogs or kittens?'

A filthy old prospector playing stud at a nearby table chuckled, ducking his head over his cards when Josh turned to glare at him. Glancing around the room, Josh had the feeling every man there was more interested in what might happen at the bar than the woman on their arm, the drink in their hand or the bet on the table. Not for the first time he noticed two men, engaged in their own activities and yet obviously together. If he had to guess, he'd say they were brothers or family at least. Same gaunt faces, same dark, watchful eyes looking furtively in his direction.

'Aw, shut up, Zack,' Josh snapped as a chill of foreboding settled on him. 'I ain't in the mood.'

He turned again to face a fresh drink, swirling it carefully around the glass as he sought to regain his calm.

'So, who's your new friend?' Zack asked.

'What?'

'The girl. You seemed reluctant to let her go. She didn't look much from what I could see but you hung on to her like a five-dollar whore. I thought maybe she had broken through that hard shell of yours and . . . '

The observation rattled Josh, but he couldn't let Zack see that. If the younger man thought Josh had any interest in the girl he would worry the fact like a dog with a bone until he did something stupid about it. It was in his blood. Just the mention of a woman had set him preening and looking around until a little *señorita* draped over a drunk at the end of the bar winked at him.

'Just like the rest of your family,' Josh commented casually. 'Maybe I should warn her about your left hook.'

'You take that back, McCabe.' An ugly sneer aged Zack's boyish good looks as he faced Josh, his stance low, arms held loose at his sides, hands curling into fists. 'I've never raised my hand to a woman and I never will.'

Zack's violent reaction to what was nothing more than banter surprised Josh. It was new, unexpected really, but being the nephew of a gang of killers Zack had a lot to prove. Josh being the man who had hunted the rest of the Lawtons down and delivered them ready for the hangman, all except Abe, was as big a score as Zack was ever likely to make.

Already the noise level had dropped and chairs scraped across muddy boards as a space cleared around the two men. Suddenly, after everything else — his near-death experience with the girl, the unwanted attention and this cat-and-mouse game with Zack — Josh wanted a fight. He really wanted to whoop Zack's tail.

Not that he would. Plenty of men in the crowd around them would like to put a bullet in the back of a Lawton, even a lesser-known and so far law-abiding member of that notorious family. The rest would certainly enjoy seeing a man-hunter take the blame, and he wasn't about to make himself a scapegoat for their dark alley antics. Probably the two strangers who had started circling like buzzards had just that on their minds.

'Take it easy, kid.' He couldn't help making a slight inclination of his head towards one of the strangers, a warning if the kid was sharp enough to notice it. 'Have another drink.'

The bartender was already pouring whiskey into a glass. He nudged it towards Zack, but instead of picking it up, Zack pushed it aside.

'You know I don't drink that gut rot,' he said, contemptuously.

'Maybe you should start.' Josh picked it up and swallowed it in one gulp while the kid glared at him.

'You fightin' or lovin', handsome?' the *señorita* with the dark eyes asked, cutting between them and wrapping her bruised arms around Zack's waist. 'Joe gets upset when customers bust the place up. It'd be a shame if you had to spend the night in jail when you could spend it with me.'

'That's a mighty persuasive argument, why don't we . . . ' Zack's smile returned as he whispered the details against her ear.

Josh settled his elbows over another fresh drink, forcing his breathing back into a steady rhythm as he glanced through the mirror hung behind the barkeep. Despite the wide angle of view it offered, he could no longer see the two strangers.

'You need to loosen up, McCabe,' Zack said, apparently losing his interest in Josh as the whore coaxed him away. 'Enjoy yourself. Live a little . . . while you still can. This place is probably as close to heaven as you'll ever get.'

5

Josh cussed under his breath. From what he had seen of the town in the hour or so he had been there, it was little more than a stopping point for people with no particular destination. The sooner he finished his business, picked up some supplies and got the hell out of there the better.

He tossed down another whiskey as he watched Zack disappear into the crowd, then he sullenly ordered a plate of stew, his tone brooking any argument when he told the barkeep to leave him a bottle and hunched over the bar to drown his sorrows.

'Buy a girl a drink, cowboy?'

Foul breath and the odour of sweat and God only knew what else filled his nostrils as he turned his head towards the speaker. The sight almost made him flinch. He had seen some sad-looking whores in his time, even felt sorry for a few of them, but this creature was easily the most used up he had ever met. A faded red dress hung from her bony frame, revealing saggy bruised breasts. The rouge on her lips seemed to have been drawn on to form a smile that had long since deserted the thin puckered mouth. She could have been thirty or fifty. It was hard to tell.

'I saw what you did for that girl out there.' She rested her hand on his arm. 'You're a brave one . . . and handsome,' she added, her gaze moving admiringly over his face.

'I didn't have much of a choice,' he said, remembering again the hand on his back that had shoved him squarely into the road. 'I don't think I did her much of a favour. It seemed to me she's as crazy as a loon. Why the hell else would a girl like that come to a place like this?'

'It takes all sorts, I guess. How about I try and explain it to you?'

Josh's flesh crawled at the suggestion

in her voice and he eased away as she pressed in closer towards him, her breathing almost stalling the breath in his throat.

'Leave him alone, Jenny,' the barkeep said, sliding a drink towards her. 'Can't you see he's had enough of a scare today without looking at your scrawny face?'

'You're right there, Joe,' someone said as several new patrons pushed up to the bar.

The insult seemed to fire her up and she emptied the glass in one gulp. 'I was like that girl once upon a time,' she shouted, wiping the back of her hand across her mouth. 'I had dreams pure as the driven snow until a smooth-talking louse marooned me in this hell-hole of a town.'

'You couldn't have been as pure as your dreams if you were travelling with a louse in the first place.'

That raised a laugh from everyone but Jenny.

'I came from a good family,' she

mumbled. 'I didn't know how good 'til they were lost to me.'

Josh sipped his drink, content now that Jenny's attention was diverted elsewhere, to just let her drunken rambling wash over him. But he couldn't help noticing tears in her eyes as she turned back to the bar and stared at her reflection in the mirror hung on the wall behind. His gaze settled on her huge blue eyes which might have been pretty against her greying hair but had long since lost their shine. For a few seconds he couldn't look away as his mind wandered back to the girl in the street. Her eyes were blue too, wide and full of wonder when she had asked him if he was an angel. Him? An angel! It was an interesting thought that made him check his reflection and immediately drop his head sullenly over his drink.

His first impression of the girl had been right, he concluded. She was crazy, or half blind, to mistake him for anything other than a devil. He ran his hand through his unkempt greying hair and across his stubble-covered chin, his feeling of contempt for the life that had chosen him burning stronger than usual.

Jenny knocked his arm as she gripped her empty glass. 'There was a time when people showed me some respect. When women envied me and men fell at my feet. My name was one of the most revered for a hundred miles.'

'What, Jenny Bones the ten-cent whore?' someone shouted.

She shook her head decisively. 'Laugh all you like, gentlemen, but one day you'll be proud to have known Eugenia Allbright.'

Josh grabbed her arm. 'You're Eugenia Allbright?'

She looked him over, smiling triumphantly as she stared him square in the eye. 'That's right,' she said with a new level of dignity.

'Hell no.' Josh winced at his next words. 'You're the woman that girl's looking for.'

'Me? Why would she be looking for me? Nobody even knows me by that name anymore.'

Josh shrugged, not knowing and not caring, as he picked up the bottle of whiskey and turned away. Two sod-busters were just vacating a small table and out of habit Josh took a seat facing into the crowd. Annoyingly, Jenny sat down opposite and pushed her glass forward. After a hesitation he poured a couple of drinks, downing one and refilling it as he wondered what the hell he was doing getting involved in business that didn't concern him.

6

Ellen had watched the big man walk away and enter a saloon. Without the support of his hand on her back, misery wobbled her chin and trembled its way right down to her knees. Unfamiliar places over-whelmed her with their constant movement and sounds. Today, with people still staring at her as they bent their heads together or talked behind raised hands, that feeling pressed in on her tenfold.

Turning, she felt her spirits lift as she recognized the name of the hotel Mr McCabe had indicated. The Majestic. Aptly named, judging by its brightly painted frontage and sparkling windows. As she approached she once again tried to smarten herself up but a tug and a smooth here and there couldn't improve her sodden appearance and before she was even through the door a voice inside boomed at her.

'Stop. You can't come in here looking like that and dripping mud all over the floor.'

With determination born out of desperation she walked forward anyway. But before she had taken more than three steps, the man behind the reception desk slammed closed his ledger and hurried to meet her, waving his arms as if to shoo her physically back into the street.

'Please, sir, I can pay.'

The clerk seemed to pay her no mind as he continued to back her towards the doors that would see her out in the street again. 'Well, that's as may be, miss, but you're not coming in here until you've gotten yourself cleaned up. You might even want to find a room in a cheaper establishment. Do I make myself clear?'

He shut the door in her face without waiting for an answer. Then, with his arms folded across his chest, he stood behind the etched glass and waited for her to leave. With tears in her eyes, she turned away and, after staring at the two dollars on her palm, she glanced along the street. It reminded her of Bluewater Creek but whereas Bluewater only had one saloon, this town had several in close proximity as well as two more hotels, which she could see, a dry-goods store and a bathhouse. Goodness only knew what else lay around the bend, but right now, she didn't care as her eyes strayed back to the bathhouse. With two dollars she should be able to get a good soak, a hot meal and still have money for a cheap room in a boarding house, if it came to that.

But Mr McCabe had told her to go the hotel. Would he be angry with her if she used the money more wisely?

Somewhere a clock chimed, her indecision see-sawing with each strike of the hour. Mr McCabe hadn't known she was starving. How could he? Surely if he had, he would have given her enough for a meal as well. Not that she would have expected it. Until she found her mother, she had no way of repaying the debt as it stood, let alone adding more to the sum.

As the clock struck four, she made her decision and with renewed determination in her step, strode towards her first destination. She would explain her decision to Mr McCabe when next she saw him and, being the kind-hearted man that he obviously was, he would understand and probably praise her for her wise thinking.

She was still nodding decisively when she entered the bathhouse and followed a sign with a crudely painted arrow that directed her through a door and into an adjoining room. Even before the door slammed behind her she had taken in the man sitting in a high chair, draped in a grey-white sheet, his face covered with a steaming towel. Standing next to him was a giant at least as tall as Mr McCabe but twice as wide with curly grey hair and a beard that hung halfway down his stomach. It all added to the illusion that he was half beast and his shirtsleeves rolled up past his elbows revealed a red undershirt that bulged with solid muscle, dwarfing the blade in his hand. As he looked her over from head to toe and back again, Ellen quaked under the intensity of a flint grey stare that turned her knees to water and her feet to stone.

'Can I do something for you, miss?' he asked in a voice as soft as a woman's.

Ellen swallowed, taking a moment to compose herself as she looked around the small room, noticing bottles of cologne, a strop, a bowl of steaming water, and some towels on the floor amidst a pile of multicoloured hair clippings. To her right was a large window on which the words *Barber Shop* were painted in reverse. As the man moved aside, she stared at her reflection in a large mirror at his back and cringed.

'Are you the owner?'

'I am. Bart Monroe's the name and

I'm a busy man, so what can I do for you?'

'My name's Ellen Cahill,' she said, holding her breath as she expected him to recognize the name. 'I need a bath.'

'Yes, you do.' He looked her over again, teeth flashing in a smile amidst the mass of his beard. 'Have you got a dollar?'

'A dollar? The sign says twenty-five cents.'

'That's for menfolk. I have to make special preparations for ladies.' He grinned. 'You are a lady, aren't you?'

The hint of ridicule in his tone shot a bolt of steel through her spine. 'Of course,' she retorted. 'It's just that . . . well, two dollars is all I have and I was hoping to get a room and a meal with that as well as the bath.'

He walked towards her, slow and steady like a cat stalking a mouse. Despite the weakness in her legs, she straightened her back even more and raised her chin. As he grasped her jaw, her hunger pangs disappeared as fear flipped her stomach every which way, setting off a chain reaction of motion that made her leap back and clutch the carpetbag to her chest.

The man chuckled. 'It's all right,' he said, holding up a towel. 'I just wanted to clean some of that mud off your cheeks and get a proper look at you.'

She took the towel and wiped it over her face, enjoying its damp warmth as she held it against her skin. Until then she hadn't realized how cold she was and as a series of shivers coursed through her she handed it back and smiled, hoping to win him over.

'Thank you. It turns out I can't afford a bath but I'm very grateful for the towel.'

His eyes twinkled, his gaze never leaving her face. 'What are you doing here?'

'I wanted a bath.'

'No, I mean, what are you doing in Bostock? You didn't come in on the stage and you already said you don't have much money. So I'm wondering, what's a pretty, educated-sounding girl

46

like you doing wandering around on her own in a town like this.'

His questions raised many of the doubts she herself had been labouring under since leaving Bluewater, but the reasons for her swift departure were still too painful to think about. With new trepidation forming a knot in her stomach, she struggled to maintain her outward show of confidence and decided to err on the side of caution.

'I'm meeting my mother here.' Ellen's spirits lifted as they always did when she talked about her mother. Anticipation swelled in her chest and chased away her uncertainties as she drew on a lifetime of longing and admiration. 'Eugenia Allbright. You wouldn't happen to know where I might find her, would you?'

Bart gave it some thought. 'I don't recognize the name.'

Ellen sighed. 'Oh well, I'll just have to wait for the sheriff to get back. Mr McCabe said he'd pass him a message, let him know I wanted to speak to him.

Maybe he'll be able to help me.'

The man in the chair pulled the towel off his face and dropped it to the floor, turning slowly to stare at her as he did so. Again she felt a chill, but it had more to do with the man's gaunt face, pale despite the heat of the recently discarded towel, than the cold and wetness gnawing at her bones. He seemed more ghostlike than flesh-and-blood human, standing and moving across the space between them to grasp her arm in a bony hand before she even realized he had moved.

Like a woman possessed, she struggled to break free, her efforts punctuated by short sharp screams that manifested more like hysterical whimpers as she bucked against his restraint. Viciously, he back-handed her across the mouth. Lightning sharp pain tore through her neck as her head whipped to the side.

Bart raised his hand to stop the next blow. 'I'll have none of that in here.'

'Do you know who I am?' the man asked.

'It wouldn't make a difference. I'll not see a woman — a girl — treated that way.'

His customer shrugged and Bart lowered his defence. The punch that followed was so quick it hardly registered before the thud that threw Bart backwards, through the glass in the door, and bloody and unconscious on to the sidewalk.

Ellen froze, then started to shake. She slumped as her legs turned to water, but the devil held her, the same way he had held her before back in Bluewater. When he had beaten her father to within an inch of death, and told him that the last thing he would see was Abe Lawton taking his little girl. And the last thing he would hear would be her begging for mercy.

She snapped back to reality now as he shook her like a rag doll.

'Did you say McCabe; Josh McCabe?'

She nodded, wondering why it felt like a betrayal but too afraid to stop herself.

'Is he a friend of yours?' he asked.

Somehow it seemed safer to say he was and again she nodded.

'Where is he?'

'I don't know.'

She should have left it at that but she panicked. Lawton didn't seem to recognize her. Why would he? He had raped several women during his weeks spent destroying Bluewater.

'He told me to wait at the hotel. I think I better do that,' she said, wanting only to be free of him; to run and never look back. 'Please, let me go.'

To her relief, if it could be called that, he smiled and loosened his grip on her arm. 'Sure. In fact, I'll walk you over there and we can wait for your friend together.'

7

Josh poured another large measure of whiskey into Jenny's glass and sat back to wait for his meal. The old whore sipped her drink before placing the glass down on the table and focusing all her attention on the amber liquid. After a few long minutes she asked: 'What's the deal with you and Zack Lawton?'

That wasn't the question he had been expecting but he answered it anyway. 'No deal. I'm trailing his brother and he's trailing me.'

'You mean you aren't helping him?'

'Helping him?' The likelihood actually amused Josh and he laughed out loud, drawing several glances. 'Lady, why would he need my help for anything other than standing still while he puts a bullet in my back?'

'I just thought . . . he doesn't seem like the other Lawtons. They're a nasty bunch. Thieves, murderers, women-beaters . . . but I don't need to tell you that. It just seemed to me that this one's different somehow. Maybe with you helping him he wouldn't have to go down that road.'

'It's in the blood. There's nothing me or anybody else can do about it.'

She sighed as though she disagreed but accepted the futility of arguing with him. 'So what's the story with the girl?'

That was the question he had been expecting and he felt himself relax. 'I don't know. She said she wanted to see the sheriff then mentioned your name. At least I guess it's you since a fancy name like Eugenia Allbright ain't all that common.'

Jenny didn't give anything away. 'Did she say anything else?'

'Not much. She was a mite shaken up.' He didn't add crazy, although he thought about it. 'I think she said her name was Ellen.'

'Ellen?' Jenny hung her head in her hands with a groan.

'Do you know her?' Josh asked, without any real interest, as he leaned back to allow a plate of steaming brown slop and grey bread to be pushed in front of him.

'It could be she's my daughter.'

'Maybe she's not so innocent after all then.'

After taking his time to soak a chunk of bread in the brown grease, Josh pushed it into his mouth, chewing and swallowing before he had time to taste it. By the time he had finished he still couldn't think of anything to say. Instead, he shrugged and concentrated on tucking into his meal, reminding himself that the girl was none of his business.

Yet he couldn't help thinking about her wide-eyed innocence and comparing her with this sad, old-before-her-time wretch who seemed intent on watching the food move from the plate to his mouth. It was unsettling to say the least and despite his gnawing hunger, the food seemed to lose whatever flavour it had. After a couple more mouthfuls he pushed the meal towards her, grimacing as she devoured it without a word, scraping the spoon on the plate until only a greasy film was left, which she licked with canine relish. To finish, she washed it down with a couple of gulps of whiskey.

Apparently satisfied, and a little embarrassed, she dabbed her wrist primly against her lips. 'Thanks. I've had a couple of bad days and . . . '

'I understand. I've been there myself a time or two.' He reached into his pocket and tossed a coin on the table. 'Maybe this'll help until you find your feet again.'

She stared at the money, her fingers twitching towards it, but she didn't touch it. Instead, she tilted her head, her eyes narrowed again in a harsh scrutiny that made the hair rise on the back of his neck and the heat drain from his face. His skin crawled as she seemed to probe his soul and then her expression softened. Damn! He had said too much: done too much. He had allowed the stupidity of a girl and the sadness of a whore to distract him and jeopardize his plans, if he understood the look of understanding in the whore's eyes.

Almost overturning his chair, he stood abruptly. 'Don't let me keep you from your work,' he said coldly, turning away as Jenny grabbed the bottle and the coin, holding on to them as though they were a pound of gold dust. 'And don't worry about the girl. I paid for a room at the hotel.'

'Why, you dirty son-of-a — '

Glass smashed and only lightning reflexes saved him from more than a gash across the fleshy part of his hand. As he crushed Jenny's wrist in his fist, the broken bottle fell away, but Jenny refused to bend under the pressure.

'You hear my warning, Mr — ' He hadn't given his name and she didn't spend long spluttering to find it. 'Mr whoever you are. You keep away from that girl, do you hear me? She's not like me. It isn't true what you said about it being in the blood. She's a good girl, raised proper, by a decent man. You do anything to her and I'll — '

'Get off him, you stupid whore.' Joe the barkeep dragged her backwards by the waist, fighting to hold Jenny as he tossed a cloth to Josh. 'I'm sorry, mister. I don't know what you said to her but whatever it was there was no call for her to act that way. I don't know what came over her but I can assure you the girls in this establishment don't attack the customers and get away with it.'

Josh sensed a dozen pairs of eyes turn on him. A dozen witnesses, probably including Zack, to report what happened next. And he had no doubt their stories would find the older Lawton's ears. Quickly, he reconsidered his initial reaction, to just shrug it off and move on to play a few hands of poker at one of the crowded tables before heading for the boarding house. The problem was, however much it irked him, he had a reputation to protect and with a long stride forward, he gripped her chin and shoved his face close to hers.

'You crazy bitch,' he shouted. 'You come near me again . . . do you understand?'

Jenny's eyes glistened with tears but Josh doubted they were conjured by a feeling of regret as her lips twisted in a mocking smile.

'You touch that girl and I'll kill you first,' she said through gritted teeth.

She screeched as Joe snatched her head back by the roots of her hair. 'Now you keep a civil tongue in your head, Jenny Bones, or you'll find yourself fighting the rats for scraps . . . if you live that long.'

Her grunt of acknowledgement carried a definite note of disdain but she held her tongue and slowly Josh lowered the threat of his hand. Wanting only to put an end to yet another scene he could do without, he focused his attention on his throbbing wound and the barkeep's cloth wrapped around it turning from grey to red.

'Have you got a doctor in this crazy-ass town?'

Joe nodded. 'Across the street from the Emporium.'

Josh recalled seeing the place on his way in. A smart two-storey building with a bunch of girls draped over the balcony, inviting passers-by to sample their wares.

'Jenny, you go with him,' Joe ordered.

She started to object.

'I ain't asking.' Joe turned his attention back to Josh as Jenny stormed off. 'After you get cleaned up, Mr McCabe, come back. Your drinks are on the house tonight.'

Josh weighed the offer as he pulled on his hat, but with blood dripping through his fingers, he wasn't inclined to over-think it. Between Zack, the girl and the whore he'd had enough excitement for one day. What he needed now was to get his hand fixed up and get a good night's sleep. Nothing else really mattered up to this point, he reminded himself. Only Abe Lawton was important. And when that show-down arrived, he'd need to be ready with a clear head and a steady hand.

8

Trailing Jenny's curses, Josh left the saloon, immediately colliding with her when she stopped dead in her tracks. As she careered headlong across the rough boards distinguishing the walkway from the road, it was only Josh's arm clamping around her waist and his hip colliding with the porch support that stopped them both spilling into the path of a horse and rider. As he straightened up, he glanced over his shoulder, relieved to see that no one had noticed his second rescue of the day.

'What the hell is your problem?' he shouted at her, the pain in his hand fuelling the anger in his tone.

She didn't answer. Didn't move. Just stared straight ahead. Gripping the porch rail so tight that her knuckles shone white in the light of the kerosene lamps burning there.

'Oh, to hell with you,' Josh said, losing the last grains of his patience.

He tried to push past but her hand whipped up, grabbing his arm in a vicelike grip that stopped him in his tracks. Without looking around at him, she pointed along the street. 'Is that her? Is that Ellen?'

Peering into the semi-darkness of a wet and dying day, it took him a moment to see the girl almost hidden behind the bulk of a man who seemed, to Josh, to be dragging rather than escorting her to wherever they were headed. But this time it wasn't the girl that interested him. Although the man was clean shaven and his hat was pulled low, he had a hint of familiarity about him. He looked a lot like Zack Lawton, or how Zack might look wearing twenty more years on his face.

'Abe,' he called out, stepping past Jenny and out into the road from which people were already scattering.

The name had the desired effect and

the man turned fully towards him. So did the girl, fear then relief showing on her face when she recognized Josh, but quickly disappearing when she was dragged in close and centre by Abe Lawton. Josh shoved his injured hand behind his back, letting the towel drop at his heels.

'McCabe. I heard you were in town,' Abe shouted. 'Are you following me?'

Josh laughed but there was no humour in it. 'You know I am. Why don't you let the girl go so you and I can get our business out of the way?'

Abe seemed to consider the option. 'I don't think so. It seems to me she's fine right where she is.'

Abe shifted his hand from her waist to flatten across her stomach, pressing her against him. The look of disgust on her face turned quickly to panic, her renewed efforts to free herself bringing a lascivious grin to Abe's face and reminding Josh, if he needed it, that Abe was a vicious bastard with women.

Whatever else happened, Josh needed

to get the girl away from him.

'Ellen, take it easy,' Josh called, keeping his tone as low and even as he could, hoping to calm her down. 'He won't hurt you. I promise you that.'

It worked, although tears glistened on her cheeks as Abe's hand rubbed over her belly, working its way lower with every motion. Behind his back, Josh felt warm blood seeping through his fingers, something else to consider as he wondered how he was going to get the girl away from Abe, then take the outlaw down. Although he despised Abe and his kind, he had to respect him as a gunman. On a good day, Josh might stand a chance against him in a showdown, but with blood slicking through his fingers . . .

'Hey, Abe, remember me?' Jenny walked steadily towards Lawton.

Surprisingly, he looked her over with genuine interest. 'Jenny, my little darlin', how've you been?'

'I've been fine. Of course that might all change if you harm my little girl.'

It was hard to say who looked more surprised, Abe or Ellen.

'That's right, Abe. That's my Ellen you've got there, my own flesh and blood.' Jenny stopped a couple of feet away, hands placed firmly on her narrow hips. 'She might even be yours. We had a lot of fun in the old days, didn't we?'

Josh watched the scene unfold with growing interest as Abe spun the girl to face him and stared down into the same wide blue eyes whose innocence had caught Josh off guard earlier. If he wanted to take Abe alive, now would be the ideal opportunity. He had never imagined Lawton could be caught off guard but the look of surprise on the outlaw's face was almost comical. But he still had hold of the girl and now Jenny also stood between Josh and his target.

Seconds passed like minutes as Josh played out half a dozen scenarios in his mind. Each one ended badly for the women. Some ended badly for him. As if signalling that time had run out, the piano stopped playing and Josh heard the creak of hinges as someone came out of the saloon behind him.

'Stay where you are, friend,' he warned without looking round.

Footfalls moved unsteadily forward, their owner mumbling drunkenly as he swaggered past Josh brandishing a half-empty bottle of rye. Josh tried to grab his arm, but missed, and the man stumbled into the road where he bumped into Jenny and sent her flying on to her hands and knees in the mud.

'Abe,' the drunk shouted. 'Uncle Abe, is that you?' He continued moving forward, swaying unsteadily on his feet. 'It is you.'

Josh narrowed his eyes at the familiar figure before him. Broad shoulders, slim waist, hair that curled over his collar. Store-bought clothes that fitted like they were hand made. Now the odds really were stacked against him.

'What the hell ... ?' Abe asked watching the drunk intently. 'Zack?'

'Sure it's me.' He reeled into Abe and Ellen, wrapping an arm around each of them as he struggled to keep his footing. 'Who's your friend?'

Abe untangled himself, having to take a step to the side to avoid a complete bear hug. In a split second, Josh saw Ellen break free. She stumbled away, backing into Jenny who was already on her feet, and Josh saw his chance. But as he reached for his gun, he hesitated.

'I thought you said you were going to kill me the next time you saw me, boy,' Abe said, goading his nephew before shoving him away.

'I did.'

'So what's changed?'

'Nothing.'

But Josh realized that something had. The drunk who had staggered from the saloon was gone and in his place stood a sober youth with hate in his eyes. Without hesitation Zack went for his gun but Abe's .45s were in his hands before either the kid or Josh could clear leather.

Josh collapsed to his knees as pain seared his thigh, the blood from his hand mingling with that spreading across his leg as he looked down the barrel of a smoking Colt, then to the man who had both himself and Zack covered despite the angle between them. Abe wasn't even looking his way, but there was no doubting he would hit his target again if he pulled the trigger. For now he seemed content to let Josh bleed while he stared down Zack, whose trembling hand suggested he realized his mistake.

9

Out of the corner of his eye, Zack saw McCabe go down, and held his breath, expecting the same fate for himself. He had known his uncle was fast with a gun but he had barely seen his hands move. Even as he stared at the barrel of the Colt aimed at his stomach, he hardly believed it. It took a few seconds for him to realize that he was still standing and that Abe was talking to him.

'I promised your pa I'd take care of you, boy. Don't make me a liar.'

A voice inside Zack's head said he should back down, walk away, if Abe would let him but . . . 'Was that before or after you killed him and Ma?'

'That was an accident. Your pa was a fool. He thought he could be something he wasn't, wanted the rest of us to be like him, a goddamn scratching-in-the-dirt, no-account farmer. I wasn't going to let him bring down the Lawton name.' Abe faltered as if he'd said more than he intended. 'It wasn't my fault what happened to him.'

Zack scoffed. 'I s'pose he ran into that knife you pulled out of his chest?'

'That's the way it was, boy.'

'And Ma? How did she end up with one of your bullets in her belly?'

'By coming at me the way you're coming at me now.'

The tension buzzed in Zack's ears. He had come too far to let Abe walk away.

'It's obvious I can't beat you in a gunfight, Abe.' Zack moved slowly to unbuckle his belt, tossing it behind him to Jenny who caught it and clutched it to her bony chest. 'But you owe me a chance to even the score. Are you man enough to fight me without your guns?'

Abe's eyes narrowed, his gaze circling the crowd growing around them. Eventually, with a small nod, he said, 'And have that man hunter you've been following around like a puppy shoot me

69

down when my back's turned?'

'We both know that's not going to happen with your weasel-faced friend standing behind him and a pistol shoved in his back.'

As the man bent and slipped Josh's gun out of its holster, Abe laughed with genuine amusement.

'Now that's better.' He holstered his guns. 'And if any of you other folks got any ideas about taking me down, forget it. I've got another friend hidden somewheres around here who'll be glad to part your everlasting souls from your worthless bodies. Now let's finish this.'

It had seemed like a good idea at the time. After all, for ten years Zack had dreamed about this moment. Abe had killed his parents and he would kill Abe. But the reality was far removed from the scenes that had played out in his mind. He had imagined they would stand face to face, that he would get the first shot in, or at least the first blow, but reality was already ringing in his ears as he lay face down in the dirt, spitting blood as he tried to shake the mist from his eyes.

His humiliation and frustration mounted as an agonizing burn seared his spine dead centre where Abe's knee dug deep, rendering him powerless to struggle as Abe's arm locked around his throat.

'You don't want this, boy,' Abe said against his ear. 'You've shown spirit and I admire you for that, but you ain't good enough to kill me and I made a promise to your pa.'

Zack struggled to free himself, but Abe's grip tightened, increasing the agony.

'Go to hell, you . . . '

He lost his breath momentarily as Abe thrust his knee forward, arching Zack's back at an unnatural angle. Lightning sharp pain split him in two, intensifying with each sadistic yank on his numbing throat. Out of the corner of his eye he spied Jenny, her eyes full of fear as she fumbled to take Zack's gun from its holster.

'Let him go. Leave him alone.' Her unyielding tone belied the shaking of her scrawny body as the gun came level. 'He deserves a chance. I ain't going to let you kill him like you killed his ma and pa.'

'Jenny, no!' Zack wasn't certain the words came out as another shaft of agony tore along his spine.

A shot boomed, unleashing chaos as folks who had been only too eager to stand and watch now ran for cover from the unseen gunman. Zack smacked face down in the mud, sucking air into his starved lungs, and glimpsed Jenny falling, blood spreading across the front of her dress as she fell backwards into the girl's arms.

Tears pricked his eyes, held back only by the anger that burned like a fuse and propelled him in pursuit of Abe. He lunged at his legs, curled his fingers around his boot and yanked. Abe wobbled but a vicious backward heel sent Zack reeling on to his back, his cheek stinging where Abe's spur had torn the flesh. But that was nothing compared to the agony another half dozen more vicious kicks inflicted to his ribs and chest.

Powerless to fight or protect himself as bones cracked and his body weakened, Zack glimpsed McCabe struggling to his feet, holding his blood-soaked leg with one hand as he brought up a gun with the other. Weasel-face was nowhere to be seen.

'Hold it right there, Abe,' Josh shouted across the distance. 'The sheriff's got your man covered.' Silence and stillness cloaked them all like a blanket. 'It's over.'

Abe laughed. 'It ain't over while I'm still breathing.' He toed Zack in the stomach one last time before turning to face the man hunter. 'Are you ready to finish it, McCabe?'

With his head spinning and his body quivering, Zack willed himself not to pass out. He had wanted to take Abe down himself, but what difference did it make who pulled the trigger as long as Abe paid? At the very least, he wanted to see it.

He glanced across at the girl, meeting her teary blue gaze as she looked up from stroking Jenny's hair. His heart clenched. The old whore was dead; her faded dress stained a deep red where the bullet had ripped into her chest.

'Throw down your guns, Abe,' Josh ordered.

Abe shook his head.

'I'm warning you . . . '

Zack heard the slap of reins, the jingle of spurs, a 'yee-haw', hoof beats closing in rapidly behind him. Abe's guns leaped into his hands, spitting fire almost simultaneously. McCabe went down, blood coming from a fresh wound to his arm. Behind him, an unlucky bystander gripped his stomach and staggered backwards into the panicked crowd.

Then Abe was running, being pulled up on to a horse that passed so close to Zack he closed his eyes and held his breath, expecting to be trampled under the pounding hoofs. But he wasn't, and as another shot boomed, he opened his eyes to see Abe almost fall from the back of the racing animal before disappearing into a veil of persistent drizzle.

Eventually, Zack's body slackened, his head lolling to the side. Abe had gotten away, but not without a bullet inside him and even that held a certain amount of satisfaction. He glimpsed McCabe, unsure whether the man hunter was alive or dead as folks moved tentatively from their hiding places. He hoped he was alive.

'You better give me that gun, miss,' someone said close by.

Zack's gaze shifted to a fat, wheezy man with a sheriff's badge pinned to his coat. Looking past him, he saw the girl on her back, her stare fixed on the smoking gun clutched between her hands. And being carried away, McCabe. Closing his eyes, Zack waited for the pain to take him into unconsciousness, but as a new set of nightmares mingled with the old, it didn't.

10

Ellen stared blankly at the bars of the cell where the sheriff had brought her after the street was cleared. She wondered whether she had been arrested. After all, she had shot a man. Maybe they'd hang her. Did they hang women? It was all she deserved, as long as Abe Lawton was dead. She shuddered. Despite everything that had happened, everything he had done to her, deep down she knew it was wrong to want a man dead. Maybe it wasn't his fault that he was the way he was. What made her think she was any better than him with a whore for a mother and a reformed gambler for a father?

'Has she said anything?' someone enquired in a hushed voice.

'Not a word. I think this one's going to turn out to be just the kind of girl you like; a real money-spinner for both of us.'

Footsteps scuffled on the edge of her subconscious and two pairs of boots stepped inside the cell. One pair, worn and dirty, she recognized as the sheriff's. The second, old but clean, she didn't recognize but her mind grasped at the possibility that they belonged to Mr McCabe. A tentative smile was already forming as she looked up but it quickly slipped as she met the penetrating gaze of a man she didn't recognize and instantly disliked, despite his beaming grin.

'How are you feeling?' the stranger asked, dropping to his haunches beside the low cot. 'How's Monte — I mean the sheriff been treating you?'

A strange mixture of smoke, sweat and cologne wafted towards her. It heightened her senses as keenly as a bottle of smelling-salts. She noticed he had a gold tooth, a scar on his chin, garters holding up the sleeves of his stained shirt. And that the smile on his lips didn't reach the corners of his close-set pale eyes.

She yanked the thin blanket, that had been placed around her shoulders earlier, tighter under her chin as if it would ward off the danger that emanated from him but even so her skin crawled.

'Don't scare her, Joe,' the sheriff warned, smiling at her over the man's shoulder.

'Why would I do that?' He rested his hand on her shoulder, his fingers squeezing slightly as he stared mesmerizingly into her eyes. 'I'm going to look after you, if you'll trust me. I'm here to help you.'

She doubted it and it was all she could do not to scream and try to make a run for it.

'Help yourself, you mean.' The new speaker entered the confined space, causing the sheriff to step aside with a grunt.

Ellen immediately liked him. He was dressed in a dark suit and his shoes were clean except for a couple of splashes of wet mud. His face, although pinched with tiredness was kind and when he smiled his eyes crinkled at the corners. When he reached out to touch her face, she noticed his hands smelled of soap, and when he looked closely into her eyes she knew she was right to trust him.

'There's no need to take that attitude, Doc,' Joe whined. 'I just came over to see what I could do for the girl. After all, her ma did work for me, God rest her soul.'

The doctor ignored him. 'It's Ellen, isn't it?' he asked.

She nodded.

'How do you feel? Are you hurt anywhere?'

She shook her head, her focus never leaving his face.

'Good.' He took her hand and guided her on to her feet. 'Then come with me.'

Without hesitation, she started to follow, but they were brought up short by the sheriff stepping across the doorway. 'Now just a minute, Doc, you can't just waltz in here and take the girl away without so much as a by your leave,' he argued.

'Why not? Is she a prisoner?'

'No, but — '

'But what?' the medic asked impatiently.

The sheriff looked at Joe.

'I was going to take her into my care,' Joe said, moving in close to the sheriff's side. 'After all, her mother did — '

'Work for you?' the doctor finished. He glanced around at Ellen and lowered his voice. 'I've seen the girls who work for you. I wouldn't let you take care of a mangy dog.'

Ellen held her breath as Joe's face turned crimson. Nervously, she gripped the back of the doctor's coat and pressed in behind him.

'You think a lot of yourself, don't you, Doc?' It was a rhetorical question and Joe didn't wait for an answer. 'Well, you just remember that I own half this town and I can get a replacement tinhorn doctor anytime. You'd do well to stay out of my business, except that which I pay you for.'

Ellen's heart sank as Joe pressed his face within a hair's breadth of the doctor's. She expected the medic to back down, wouldn't have blamed him, but instead she felt his back straighten as he refused to budge an inch from the threats.

'Maybe you need me and maybe you don't,' he said, 'but I'm guessing you'd sooner not have any trouble with the bounty hunter.'

Joe's eyes narrowed. 'McCabe? What's he got to do with anything? Ain't he dead?'

The doctor shook his head. 'He's waiting for the girl. Do you want to be the one to tell him why she couldn't come? Do you want me to tell him that you, Sheriff,' he said, switching his attention, 'were about to sell his niece to the town's whore master?'

'McCabe's niece? I thought she was a

stray.' The sheriff shuffled nervously, wiping his jowls with his hand as he looked between the girl, the doctor and Joe. 'You told me she was — '

'Shut up, Monte. He's bluffing. She ain't McCabe's niece,' Joe snapped. He shoved the sheriff out of the cell and stepped aside with an untidy flourish of his arm. 'Go ahead, take her. Like I said, I was just trying to help.'

Ellen relaxed, sticking so close to the doc as he strode out that she risked tripping him. She almost screamed when her arm was grabbed before she was clear of the small grey cell and the oppressive atmosphere inside.

'Ellen,' Joe said with surprising gentleness, 'I'll see that your ma's buried proper. Maybe after the funeral, when things settle down, you'll come and see me. I'll have one of the girls bundle up her belongings for you. She'd want you to have them, I'm sure.'

For the briefest of moments, the usual flush of excitement and pride welled up inside her as she pictured

Eugenia Allbright, beautiful actress. Then she pictured the whore with the painted smile and the faded dress. For the first time since the horror in the street, choking emotion welled in her chest, damming her throat and bringing wetness flooding into her eyes. But this time the tears weren't for her father or her mother or Mr McCabe.

Outside in the street, the doctor wrapped his arm comfortingly around her shoulder. 'That's it, let it all out. You're safe now.'

She buried her face against his chest. After a few seconds, he peeled her loose and held her at arm's length, a serious look on his face as he stared intently at her.

'I knew your mother, Ellen. She had fallen on hard times but she never gave up hope of seeing you.'

'Me? You mean she mentioned me?'

'She told me all about your life in Bluewater. How she left you with your pa so you could have a normal life. Don't let what's happened here today ruin that dream.'

The news knocked her sideways. She wanted to ask him a hundred questions but couldn't think where to start. Already he was talking again.

'Whatever else you do, keep away from Joe. Your mother would have wanted that above all else. He's an evil man. Do you understand?'

She nodded, not needing to be told twice.

11

Josh stared blankly at the whitewashed ceiling. The room where he had been brought smelled of fresh paint and linen washed in lye soap. Mingling with the heat of a fire that had been banked high and stoked often, it turned his already queasy stomach. Jeez, he hurt.

The doc, a young man with more enthusiasm than experience, had got the bullets out of his arm and leg, cleaned and tended the wounds and put him in a not uncomfortable cot to recover with a good dose of laudanum to dull the pain. And yet he winced. Not at his own hurt but at that of the girl who sat with her head in her hands, crying gently against the blankets covering him.

Through the fog clouding his mind, he remembered her name was Ellen. She had been with him since the doc brought her over from the jail and she had rushed to his side, holding on to his hand as if she would drag him back from the gates of Hell if the Devil dared try and take him. Or maybe she was hoping he would drag her back from the gates of Hell after what the doctor had told him about the sheriff and Joe the barkeep.

With an effort, he slid his hand across the coverlet and touched her. He realized he must have fallen asleep at some point because her hair was dry and it felt clean and soft. When she looked up, wiping away tears from her bright-blue eyes, her face was clean and pretty and he realized that she was younger than he had imagined. About fifteen maybe. But that wasn't what made his heart clench in a painful knot. He wanted to look away, but the resemblance was uncanny. Covered in mud as she had been, he hadn't been able to see it before, but now more than ever he felt his hatred of Abe Lawton rise to choke him. He cleared his throat and tried to speak but only managed a croak.

Reaching across to a table beside the bed, the girl splashed water into a bowl then brought a wet cloth to his lips. She squeezed it gently, trickling cool liquid into his mouth.

'Thank you for saving me. I know I didn't deserve it,' she said as if the words had been waiting to jump out. 'I didn't mean to bring him to you — Lawton, I mean. I was so afraid when he grabbed me and I remembered every-thing that happened before and — '

'Shush, it's all right. Lawton and I go way back. Nothing you did caused what happened.' He was going to leave it at that but the relief that flooded her face made him feel better and he added, 'You were very brave, doing what you did. I should be thanking you for saving my life.'

'I'm not brave. I was scared when I saw you on the ground, all that blood . . . I thought you'd die like my pa.'

'It'll take more than a couple of bullets to kill me.' He didn't add that fever might still take him if it got hold. 'I'm sorry about your mother. How are you holding up, Ellen?'

She sucked on her lip, turning her chin into her shoulder as tears welled again in her eyes. 'I don't know what I'm going to do. I've lost everything.'

Surprising himself, Josh touched her cheek. It was strange how something about this girl made him care what happened to her. Maybe it was the absence of fear, or the lack of contempt she showed towards him or, right now, just light-headedness caused by loss of blood. Whatever it was, he rolled his eyes towards a ladder-back chair standing in the corner.

'My coat,' he said. 'There's money in an inside pocket. Take what you need.'

'I don't want your money. The doctor says I can stay here, look after you until you're well enough to leave, keep house for him while his wife's away. I meant I've got nothing. No family. No plans for the future. That man . . . ' She waved her arm wildly towards the window. 'Lawton. He took everything from me. My home. My family.'

Her words touched a nerve, opening old wounds that brought a bitter taste to his mouth and made his next words sound harsher than he intended.

'He left you with your life. There's nothing more valuable than that, especially when you're young. It could just as easily have been you dead in the street as your — ' He stopped himself from pouring salt into an open wound and turned his head so he could see the cot next to his. 'How's the kid?' He felt her stiffen and turned his attention back on her. 'Is he hurt bad?'

'He's alive.'

There was a coolness in her tone that he didn't expect and her eyes narrowed as she glanced across at the sleeping man.

'He's got a couple of broken ribs and his shoulder was dislocated. The doctor's keeping him asleep. He says he's got a concussion but he should live.'

Josh shook his head regretfully. During the months when Zack had been trailing him his mistrust of the kid had always been tinged with something he couldn't quite put his finger on. The younger Lawton had never seemed to have the hardness about him that his uncles did. Over a couple of glasses of beer in a saloon the two of them could have been old friends, except for the needling. The kid was always at him, more talk than action really. At the time Josh hadn't seen it that way but it all made sense now. Inexperienced as he was, the kid had probably just been using Josh to find Abe. Maybe he had even been hoping that Josh would back him in his play. If so, that hadn't worked out well for him.

'I hope he does,' he muttered.

Tiredness weighed heavy on Josh's lids now but he fought against it. The girl was looking at him intently, her brow furrowed with worry. He chuckled. She shouldn't be wasting her concern on an old man like him. Pure orneriness would pull him through, it had before, but Zack . . . a beating like that could take more out of a man than just his physical strength.

'You should sit with him. It seems to me you two have a lot in common,' he mumbled as he slipped into oblivion. 'It might even help to keep those ghosts away.'

★   ★   ★

Ellen sat at McCabe's side for a long time after he fell asleep. Somehow, she couldn't make herself move to the other bed and its silent, battered and unmoving patient. Despite his vulnerable appearance, he was a Lawton and that was all she could really think about. A flesh-and-blood relation to the man who had killed her father and been responsible for the death of her mother.

But Mr McCabe seemed to have a real affection for 'the kid' as he called him. Did that mean she couldn't trust

Mr McCabe either? She thought back to the snippets of conversation she'd heard while she was in jail. The sheriff's opinion hadn't been very flattering. *McCabe*, he had said to a man she knew now to have been Joe, *was a killer. Trouble just waiting to happen. No better than the outlaws he brought in for payment. Joe had agreed, adding that if it hadn't been for the bounty hunter, Jenny would still be alive.*

Ellen sighed and rubbed her eyes as pure weariness settled over her. It was hard to know whom to trust, but with Mr McCabe and Lawton bedridden and the doctor short-handed, she had a few days to make up her mind what she would do next.

12

When Zack woke the room was bright. A breeze stirred the air, and as he tried to accustom his eyes to the light he made out the profile of a girl standing by the window. As he watched, her chest rose and fell with each gentle flutter of the lacy curtains covering the window. She seemed to be crying.

'Maggie?'

It was hard for him to concentrate and his eyelids closed under the weight of the effort, leaving his head to throb and his body to ache.

When he opened his eyes again, the girl's face was directly above his and he found himself looking into bright-blue eyes. He noticed her cheeks were scrubbed to a rosy pink and her hair shone as bright as the sunshine that was cutting a swath between them. Sure, she was pretty, but she wasn't Maggie and the realization of where he was and what had happened hit him like a sledgehammer.

'Water,' he managed to mutter.

Her lips moved in speech but he struggled to understand whatever she was saying. His mind lingered in a fog. His ears seemed blocked so that only an indistinct stream of sound swirled around him. She stretched to the side, fussing with something before turning back to him. It was a glass of water and as she pressed it to his lips he forced himself to concentrate.

'Don't try to talk,' she was saying. 'I'll go and tell the doctor you're awake.'

'No,' he managed to say on a gasp before she got up to leave. 'Stay . . . please.'

He tried to reach out but searing pain stopped him. He attempted to touch his ribs but his arm wouldn't move. The doc had wrapped him up tight but it was difficult to tell what injury the bandages were protecting. His whole body felt as if it was being pulled apart by a couple of Montana broncos.

Against his will he remembered Abe's boot pounding him like a hammer.

'How long has it been since . . . ?'

'A couple of days.'

'Are you the girl from the street?'

She hesitated. 'You're very sick. I should fetch Doctor Morris so he can give you something for the pain.'

'He can't give me anything for my kind of pain.'

She looked at him quizzically.

'What's your name?' he asked.

She hesitated. 'Ellen. Now close your eyes and try to go back to sleep.'

He didn't need telling twice. Already the throbbing ache was consuming him, dragging him back into a nightmare world full of ghosts that seemed more real to him than the girl sitting by his bed.

★ ★ ★

Ellen squirmed and covered her ears with her hands, wishing she were anywhere else but alone in the house with Zack Lawton. It had only been five days but Mr McCabe was already up and with the doctor's help had gone to see the sheriff. A rumour had reached them that Abe Lawton was still in the area and although she was frightened she had assured both men that she was more than capable of sitting with Zack. But in all honesty, although his body was healing, his mind seemed to be stuck in a series of nightmares he couldn't break free of and she was finding it harder to deal with the torment.

'Please, be quiet,' she said, more out of frustration than any hope that he would. 'Please.'

It made no difference and she was tempted to wake him, but the doctor had said sleep would be the best medicine and she trusted him even if it meant she had to care for a man she wanted no part of. A pang of guilt made her nibble on her already chewed lip. Zack hadn't done anything to her but she couldn't find it inside herself to feel anything except dislike. Even Mr McCabe had noticed and tried to soothe her unease by reminding her that Zack had actually saved her from Abe Lawton and had been intent on killing his uncle, but it made little difference. He was a Lawton.

With random words gushing from his mouth, making no sense as they mingled with anguished moans, she wrung out a cloth and pressed it to his forehead and cheeks for the hundredth time. It seemed to calm him and in turn she too relaxed. It had been a long day, and with the afternoon losing its brightness, she turned her gaze to the window and wondered when Mr McCabe would return.

'He's coming,' Zack said, drawing her attention.

'I know, it's just . . . '

He stared more through her than at

her. 'He's coming,' he said clearly. 'You need to run.'

She laughed. 'From Mr McCabe?'

'From Uncle Abe. Get away from here, as fast and as far as you can.'

The ferocity of his words frightened her but she gathered her wits, telling herself he was just dreaming. 'It's all right. He's coming.'

'Yes, he is. He's coming for me. He won't let anything stand in his way.'

A shiver trickled down her spine. 'Abe Lawton's gone. He won't show his face back here, not with Mr McCabe nearby.'

'He can't save you. Uncle Abe killed my ma and pa, he'll kill you and McCabe too if you don't run.'

He seemed to be wide awake: as lucid as she was. Staring into eyes filled with genuine fear, she shuddered, as if someone had walked over her grave. Nervously, she looked towards the door then the window, as if expecting to see Abe Lawton there. Not a soul wandered the street.

'It's all right, go back to sleep. I'll tell Mr McCabe when he gets back. He'll know what to do.'

He screamed like a woman, sending her reeling backwards. She held her chest, feeling her heart beating wildly beneath her fist as she watched him struggle to get out of bed.

'There ain't nothing a preacher can do against a murderer. He'll shoot him down. Cut his heart out. It's too late, Maggie. He's here. Run,' he shouted, his face turning ugly with emotion as he swayed towards her. 'Run!'

Without even thinking, Ellen lunged for the door and clawed at the handle, his fear driving her mindlessly away from the invisible danger. Behind her, something crashed and she heard glass break. Glancing over her shoulder, she saw him struggling on his one good hand and his knees in a puddle of water. Whatever strength he had momentarily found was slipping away, his half-naked, bruised and battered body turning limp as the nightmare passed and he succumbed to weakness.

It was hard not to imagine his pain and, against her own reasoning, she went back to him. Despite the revulsion his touch caused in her, somehow she managed to help him back on to the bed, almost laughing as she tucked the bed coverings around him. What had she been thinking, running like that? He was sick. If Abe Lawton had been standing next to the bed, Zack wouldn't have recognized him. And he'd called her Maggie, presumably someone he knew from his past, if nightmares worked that way. The thought sobered her. He had seemed genuinely afraid for her, whoever she was, and his concern endeared him to her.

She shook herself. Nightmares couldn't change her feelings towards him or his uncle.

'I gave him a real good beating, didn't I?'

She stiffened as she recognized the voice, then recoiled as she laid eyes on the gaunt face, almost silver in its glistening paleness. If he had seemed ghostlike before, Abe Lawton looked literally dead on his feet now. It all seemed at odds with the glassy brightness of his eyes. The bones in his hand looked close to coming clean through the skin as he clasped his lifeless arm across his body. Dried blood covered his coat-sleeve from shoulder to wrist and as he leaned heavily against the doorframe and grimaced at her she wondered what was keeping him on his feet.

'Have you come to finish what you started?' She tried to sound calm and not let the wobble in her knees show in her voice, but it did anyway. 'Or are you here to see the doctor?'

'I need some supplies out of that medicine cupboard behind you. Fill this.' He reached into his pocket and pulled out an empty flour-sack which he threw on to the bed. 'Do as I say and then I'll be on my way.'

Ellen stood rooted to the spot with her mind spiralling in a dozen different directions. Somehow, she didn't comprehend his meaning even though he continued to stare at her.

'Don't think a little nick like this . . . ' He squeezed his arm and half-grimaced, half-grinned. 'Don't think I'm any less dangerous than I was before. Get me the supplies.'

She broke into action, pulling out bottles and bandages at random. When they were tucked inside the bag she tied the top and dropped it back on to the bed.

'Hand it to me.'

After a hesitation she picked it up, holding it at arm's length and moved reluctantly around the bed. With a grin he snatched it from her and tucked it inside his coat as he reeled unsteadily against the doorframe.

'Now wake up Zack' he ordered, fumbling to take his gun from its holster. 'I want him to know it was me that killed him.'

13

'I'm awake. Let the girl go, Abe.'

Ellen flinched as Zack's fingertips brushed her arm. In the confines of the cramped sickroom there was nowhere she could go and she continued to stand between him and Abe.

'Move aside, girlie,' Abe said, motioning with a flick of his chin. 'I intend to kill my nephew and not lose any sleep about it, so don't think I won't kill you just as easily.'

'Do as he says, Ellen.'

Ellen's gaze pinned itself on the gun, which wobbled in his hand, before rising up to meet the hard stare that sent an uncontrollable shake rattling through her. Her breathing laboured under the weight of emotion rolling within. She recalled Abe Lawton standing over her pa, smoke curling from the muzzle of that same gun as he spat on the battered and broken body of a once strong man. Her fingers stroked the palms of her hands, imagining that the dampness there was her mother's blood on them. Finally, as Abe pushed himself unsteadily away from the door frame, she imagined his hands on her, tearing at her clothes, holding her down, hurting her . . .

'You don't remember me, do you?' she asked, overcome with a need to confront him.

He pursed his lips as he looked her over. 'Sure, I do. You're the girl from the street.'

She shook her head. 'From before that. In Bluewater. You killed my pa and — ' She couldn't finish with the memories clamping around her heart like an iron band.

'I killed a lot of men in Bluewater . . . and pleasured a lot of . . . ' His feverish gaze devoured her as he chose his words, 'pretty girls. A man don't remember every fly he swats or the horses he rides.' He grinned. 'What is it you're after? Revenge? Or maybe, since your ma was a whore, you've come to collect payment for your services?'

His taunting brought all her humiliation boiling to the surface, evaporating her ire as tears threatened to unravel her childish defiance. She clenched her teeth to stop them chattering but it didn't help.

'So which is it? I ain't got all day.'

'I want my life back,' she announced on a whimper.

He shook his head with mock sympathy. 'There ain't any use pining for what's gone. Look at Zack there. He's waited nearly his whole life to kill me and where's it got him? Nowhere. In the end he'll be dead and I'll still be robbing, killing and whoring. And just so's you know, when I'm feeling up to it, you're the first dove I'll be visiting.'

'Then kill me now.'

'And waste all that promise? Why, I bet Joe'll be able to charge two — maybe three dollars for a turn with a pretty thing like you.'

'You're the Devil.'

'Yes, I am.' He had been steadily slouching as he spoke, but now he wiped the back of his hand across his glistening forehead and pulled himself up proudly. 'Now step aside. I ain't funnin' any more. Last chance, girlie.'

Chance. That was the only word she heard. Her eyes went again to the gun pointed right at her middle. Then to his blood soaked arm hanging limply at his side, then back to his hand, which seemed too weak to pull the hammer back with his thumb. And last of all to the grin that twisted his already contorted expression as pain showed in every line of his grey skin.

Whether it was anger, hope or Zack's fingertips pawing at her back she couldn't say, but she lunged at Abe, throwing her whole weight behind a guttural scream. The gun clattered to the floor as they crashed out into the hall and landed in a heap on the floor. Despite his obvious weakness he was still stronger than she was and as she fought to keep astride him, he managed to shove her off.

She hit face down, feeling pain explode in her cheek, but it didn't matter as his hand clasped the back of her dress. His touch acted like a blast of dynamite inside her and she exploded into a whole new frenzy of kicking and bucking. This time she wouldn't let fear and naivety hold her still. She would fight him tooth and nail and if he killed her, well, so be it.

As he yanked her backwards she glimpsed a hallstand half-full of walking-canes. Reaching out she grasped one and, as Abe spun her around to face him, she lashed out. The gnarled stick hit him on his useless arm, tearing a pained yelp from him and freeing her as he grasped for his injured limb.

Breathing hard, she raised the cane again but held it in check. 'I'm going to kill you.'

'You little bitch. I'm going to wring your neck.'

He started towards her, predator to

prey, but he was unsteady on his feet and this time she didn't back away. When she hit him again, he stumbled. One more strike and he went to his knees. After that, all she remembered was his screams and a hand on her arm stopping the onslaught on a man who had long since grown too weak to fend off her vengeful blows and succumbed to deathlike unconsciousness.

14

'Ellen, stop. He's finished.'

Through her breathless rage, she recognized Zack's shallow voice and half-turned to continue her assault, but on him. Already he had released her arm and collapsed to his knees, head hanging, his hand pressing against the wall for support as the effort drained him. But as she raised the cane, his gaze came up to meet her, stopping her dead with both its helplessness and hopelessness.

'Whatever he did to you, don't let hate turn you into something you're not. I've been on that path a long time, Ellen, and Abe's right about one thing, it doesn't lead to anywhere good.' He hesitated, as if judging the impact of his words, then added: 'Even a man like McCabe knows that deep down.'

She hated him for speaking to her

that way, for being the voice of reason in an unreasonable world. But he was right and she realized she had been wrong. Zack wasn't like Abe Lawton. She could see it now that pent-up anger and frustration no longer blinded her. Zack was like her: haunted by a past he could do nothing to change.

'Ellen . . . '

He reached out a hand but she shrugged it off. 'I'll run and fetch Mr McCabe,' she said.

The cane clattered to the roughly boarded floor as she sped past Zack and outside into the half-light of the dying day, taking in huge gasps of revitalizing air as she ran along the main street and mounted the steps leading to the sheriff's office. Without knocking, she rushed inside. McCabe and the sheriff were seated drinking coffee on opposite sides of the lawman's desk.

Both men stared at her when she burst in. Despite the heavy bandage bulging under his pants, it was McCabe who came awkwardly to his feet and directed her with his good arm to take his chair.

'Abe Lawton,' she gasped. 'He's at the house.'

Both men exchanged troubled glances.

'Alone?' the sheriff asked.

'Zack's there. I knocked him out.'

'Who? Zack?' McCabe asked, alarm ringing in his voice.

'No, Abe. He's hurt. His arm's all bloody and useless.'

The sheriff burst into life, sending his chair clattering against the wall in his haste to shift his bulk. Tearing open a drawer, he pulled out a new-looking six-shooter and fumbled fresh rounds into the empty chambers.

'I'll take care of this,' he said, grabbing a sweat stained derby off a hook by the door.

Josh grabbed the crutch standing against the desk. 'I'll come with you.'

The sheriff looked about to decline the offer, but instead he shrugged. 'All right, if you can keep up. You too, young woman, come out of there.'

Ellen hesitated, preferring the safety of the jail-house to anywhere within spitting distance of Abe Lawton.

'I ain't in the habit of leaving the office door unlocked while it's unattended, so unless you want to spend some more time in a cell, you'll get outside now.'

The thought of the bars and the grey walls pressing in on her were enough incentive and she followed the men, staying close while the sheriff locked the heavy wooden door. When McCabe instructed her to wait there for them, she didn't argue. Just the idea of seeing them bring Abe Lawton back to the jailhouse, conscious, unconscious, dead or alive was enough to make her tremble with panic.

Watching the men walk away, she almost jumped out of her skin when a hand tapped her on the arm. Like a cat, she spun ready to strike, only just stopping before she made a terrible mistake and attacked the doctor.

'Ellen, what are you doing here? I

saw you running. What's wrong?'

She relaxed a little, although her gaze returned to follow the backs of Mr McCabe and the sheriff as they headed down Main Street.

'I had to fetch Mr McCabe,' she said, turning her full attention on the physician when the two men were no longer in sight. 'Abe Lawton came back. He wanted medical supplies and then he tried to kill Zack and I hit him. I don't know if I killed him.'

Ellen felt the tension rise again, heard it in the near-hysterical pitch of her babbling. Through a confusion of people gathering down the street, all eager to know what was happening, she could already see Abe Lawton being dragged along by the sheriff as Mr McCabe and Zack limped along behind. Just the sight of him made the panic rise in her chest and her feet itch to run.

'And Zack? Is he all right?' the doctor asked.

She pointed along the street. 'He's

coming along with them now.'

Without another word, Morris sprinted to meet up with the group. Again Ellen lapsed into melancholy. She watched as the men approached, hampered some-what by the jeering crowd which was growing around them. Abe Lawton was fighting weakly against the lawman. Mr McCabe was supporting Zack, or vice versa. The doctor waved his arms wildly and seemed to be giving orders to all of them.

Ellen waited and speculated what would happen now. Abe Lawton would hang. Mr McCabe would leave town, probably with Zack in tow, and the doctor's wife would get back from visiting her sick relative. And where would that leave Ellen?

She struggled to order her thoughts and control the mix of emotions bubbling inside her. Her father had always told her not to waste time on feeling sorry for herself, to look for the brighter side of a dark situation, but no amount of searching seemed able to lift her out of the grip of despair that sporadically crushed her then let her go in a whirl of confusion.

Dismally, she continued to stare along the street, unseeing and temporarily blinded by the flames licking from barrels of tar, set alight early as word spread of the imminent capture of Abe Lawton.

'Ellen, it's good to see you again.'

She sucked in a choking breath at the sound of Joe's voice. During their brief encounter he had frightened her only slightly less than Abe Lawton. Just the sight of him made her want to scream and run but, just as before with Abe Lawton in the barbershop, she found herself paralysed with fear.

'I see they caught Abe Lawton,' Joe said, conversationally. 'It seems like just about everybody's watching the procession.'

His fingers clamped over her mouth, his arm wrapping around her waist like a metal band before there was anything she could do about it. Her heels scraped across the plankwalk, banged down a step, then scuffed across rutted ground littered with trash as she was dragged into a side alley and away from prying eyes.

15

It was almost over.

Josh poured himself another cup of coffee from the pot on the stove in the jailhouse and sat down with an involuntary sigh. The events of the past half hour were starting to take their toll on him and although he would have enjoyed antagonizing the sheriff, who paced impatiently while he waited for the doc's diagnosis, he was satisfied just to remain upright, to watch and listen to the argument between medic and lawman.

'Sheriff, I told you to let me look him over before you dragged him in here.'

'And I told you that I wasn't letting Abe Lawton get away twice. Now quit your whining, Doc, and tell me how bad he is? Will he survive until the hanging?'

From his kneeling position beside the

low cot in the cell where Abe Lawton had been dropped like a side of beef, Doctor Morris looked up and scowled. 'He's running a fever and his arm's infected. I'd say no, not — '

'Damn it!'

'Sheriff!' The doctor's indignation was apparent even from that one word. 'You don't have to sound so disappointed.'

'Well, hanging a man like that in my town would be a lesson to the rest of them no-good dead-beats to stay away.'

The sheriff cast a glance back towards Josh and Zack. Josh stifled a chuckle.

'You seem sure he'll hang,' the doc opined, nudging the sheriff's arm so that the lantern swung back over his patient. 'What if the judge and jury find him innocent?'

The sheriff laughed uproariously. 'You're crazy, Doc.'

Morris shrugged and nodded his agreement.

Against expectations, Abe Lawton

moaned as he came back to consciousness, his eyes rolling as he struggled to focus on the faces crowded around him.

'I ain't planning on dying,' he said through clenched teeth. 'Patch me up, Doc. It's your duty.'

The medic shook his head. 'It's not that simple. Your arm's infected. It's spreading and there's . . . nothing I can do to stop it.'

Josh sensed he was holding something back and tilted his head with more interest.

'I don't believe you. Spit it out, Doc,' Abe demanded, albeit feebly.

Morris sighed. 'The only chance you've got is if I take the arm off, stop the spread of — '

'No!' Abe lashed out but the sheriff moved with surprising speed to grab his raised hand in mid-air.

'Now, you just take it easy. The doc knows what he's talking about.' A barely concealed smile twitched the corner of the lawman's mouth as he looked pointedly at the doctor. 'Like he said, it's your duty to try and save him. Ain't that right, boys?'

Suddenly, Josh felt tired. Not just bone weary but mentally exhausted. He had been chasing Abe Lawton for fifteen long years and soon it would all be over. One way or another, the man who had started him on this lonesome trail that had become his life would be dead. Did it matter whether he died publicly at the end of a hangman's rope or passed away quietly in a jail cell?

Josh looked to Zack, who sat quietly behind the sheriff's desk. The kid hadn't looked up from watching his own fingers drum on the ink-stained blotter since they'd entered. Whether he hadn't heard, didn't care or, like Josh, just didn't know the answer was impossible to say.

'What do you think, Zack?' Josh asked. 'He's your family.'

Still nothing.

'It ain't up to him,' Abe shouted from his cell. 'He ain't been no family o' mine since the day he run off with his tail between his legs. He was yeller then and he's yeller now. I won't have no coward deciding what happens to me.'

Zack's head came up slowly, his narrow-eyed glare finding Abe between the bars. 'I think the folks he caused hurt to deserve to see him get a fair trial . . . then watch him dance on the gallows.'

'You pissant little sodbuster!' Abe yelled. 'If I have to crawl back from the gates of Hell I'll kill you. You too McCabe. And that girl. I'll — '

A loud thud silenced him and set the doctor to fussing and tutting again.

'Do what you need to do, Doc,' the sheriff instructed, kneading the knuckles of his free hand against his belly. 'It'll be at least two weeks before the circuit judge comes through. You make sure this sack o' shit lives that long or I'll arrest you for obstructing justice.'

The sheriff's absurd threats amused Josh less than usual. Suddenly tired of the whole situation, he finished his coffee and banged his cup on the desk, feigning a sheepish apology as all eyes turned on him. His business here, in this town, was almost finished. Things hadn't quite turned out the way he expected, since he wouldn't be collecting the $10,000 bounty on Abe Lawton, but finally justice would be served and he would see the outlaw hang. The Lawtons' long reign of terror was over. After more than twenty years, folks could sleep in their beds at night and not worry whether they'd wake up in the morning.

He pushed up from his seat and wrestled the crutch he was using into a semi-comfortable position under his armpit. 'Justice is all any of us wants. Justice and some peace,' he commented. 'Are you coming, kid?'

Zack looked up and sighed as he pushed the chair away from the desk and got shakily to his feet. 'I guess so.'

'Will you boys be moving on now?' the sheriff asked with a hint of expectation.

'I can't speak for the kid,' Josh said, 'but as soon as I can sit a horse I'll be heading out.'

'What about you?' the sheriff asked Zack.

'Same, I guess. Me and McCabe got a lot of catching up to do now Abe's taken care of.'

The sheriff raised an eyebrow. 'Is that so? Well, I wish you luck with that, Mr Lawton. So far as I can tell, McCabe ain't the kind of man who likes 'catching up' as you put it.'

Zack shrugged amiably. 'We'll see.'

Josh settled his hat on and headed outside, stopping on the raised plankwalk while he waited for Zack to follow. 'It sounds like I might need a drink. Do you feel like a beer or maybe something a bit stronger?' he asked as the kid emerged into the near darkness.

'Nope.' He wrapped his arm around his ribs. 'I feel all in.'

'Let's go back to the doc's, then. I'm sure Ellen will want to know we've got that bastard locked up.'

They walked side by side back along Main Street, attracting a mixture of curious, grateful and contemptuous stares from those folks still loitering to discuss the day's events. Passing a general store, Josh glimpsed his own image and then Zack's in the window. Propped up by the crutch and with his arm in a sling, Josh looked as decrepit as he felt. Zack appeared no better with his face still bruised and swollen and his body stooped like an old man's.

Josh chuckled wryly, drawing Zack's attention with his sudden outburst.

'What's funny?'

'Nothing. I was just thinking I was no older than you when all this began.' He became serious. 'Chasing outlaws sure wasn't the life I planned on living.'

'I guess if it hadn't been for Abe, you and Maggie would have a passel of kids by now and you'd still be preaching and teaching school.'

Josh almost pulled up short but managed to overcome his surprise. It wasn't in him to give too much away about himself and, dredging his memory, he couldn't remember ever telling anyone about that part of his past. Even after all these years, what had happened was still too vivid, too painful to share. He had shut the door on the past, the good times and what-ifs, the day he rode out of Bluewater Creek.

Unexpectedly, anger started to rise in his chest. After all this time, he couldn't even picture Maggie's face.

'So, what are you going to do now?' he asked Zack as they neared the doc's house. 'Seems to me all you wanted was to see Abe get what he deserved for killing your folks.'

Zack considered for a second or two. 'I might go home for a while, at least the place I always think of as home. I need to let her know I kept my promise.'

'Sounds like a good idea. Who is she? Your sweet-heart?' Josh teased.

Zack looked sideways at Josh, as if the question surprised him, then shrugged. 'A lady. A real fine lady. She took me in after my folks were killed.' He closed his eyes. 'I can still see her face. She was young, about the age I am now, with gold-coloured hair, blue eyes and a smile that could light up midnight.' He inhaled, opening his eyes to give Josh a measured look. 'And she always smelled like honeysuckle. You remember that, don't you?'

Josh felt a jolt, like someone had punched him in the gut. Maggie's face came back to him as easily as if he'd seen her only a few minutes before. He breathed deep as he realized he'd been holding his breath. He looked hard at Zack, harder than he'd ever done before, and shook his head. Why hadn't he seen it sooner? But why should he have? The kid was only five or six years old back then, the last time he'd seen him, still a little shy and unsure of himself around the man of the house. Until a few days ago Josh had assumed that that boy was dead, that Zack was just another Lawton dogging his tail, waiting for the chance to kill the bounty hunter who had delivered his family to the hangman.

'You're . . . you were Zack Brown?' he asked, still struggling to believe it.

Years of bottled-up grief and rage exploded inside him and Josh's crutch clattered to the plankwalk, his fist stinging as it collided with Zack's cheek. The blow unbalanced the younger man, saving him from a second punch as he lost his footing and crashed on to his back in the dirt. Josh tried to follow through, but without the crutch he fell on to one knee, unable to manoeuvre quickly enough to catch Zack as he crawled backwards out of reach.

'What's wrong with you, McCabe? We did it. We got Abe for what he did to her.'

Josh shook his head, tasting blood in his mouth where his teeth had punctured his lip when he fell. He spat into the dirt, his face so contorted with hatred he found it difficult to speak. 'If you hadn't come to Bluewater Abe never would have come looking for you. She'd be alive. You killed her.'

'No. I loved her. She wanted to be my ma. That day, the day it happened, we were on our way to the schoolhouse to see you. She was going to tell you . . . said you had to know the truth.'

'She knew? I don't believe it. Even she wouldn't have taken in one of your kind.'

'I was just a boy. My parents had been slaughtered before my eyes. She wanted me to have a second chance. Maggie thought it was better if no one knew my real name. She thought if people did they'd treat me different. That if Abe found out where . . . '

Josh wasn't listening. He didn't need to. 'You're a Lawton. There ain't no second chances for the likes of you. There ain't no cleansing bad blood.'

'What are you saying? You know me. I've been dogging your tail for months. If I was like them I could have killed you a half a dozen times.'

128

Josh swallowed the truth down, too stubborn to admit it. 'That's one mistake you might regret.'

Zack shook his head wildly.

Someone passed Josh his crutch and he hauled himself up. 'Stay away from me, Lawton. There isn't a price on your head yet, but that might not stop me killing you on sight.'

16

Several hands helped Zack to his feet and across to the plankwalk where he sat down heavily on the step. He thanked them as he watched McCabe limp away down the street to the doc's house, wondering whether to follow. As he rubbed his cheek and waited for the pounding in his head to lessen, he decided against it. McCabe's outburst hadn't been the triumphant celebration he had been expecting but if he knew one thing about the bounty hunter, it was that he was a man of his word. For the time being, at least, Zack would give him his space.

Behind him, coming from the saloon, the strained notes of a bawdy tune banged mercilessly on a tin-panny piano, intensifying the thumping in Zack's head. He saw McCabe emerge from the doc's carrying his saddlebags, watched him cross the street to the hotel without a sideways glance and disappear inside. Shakily, Zack pushed to his feet, using the wall for support as he staggered, nearly ending up in the dirt again as he fought to steady his reeling world.

'Hey, watch it!'

He grabbed wildly in the direction of the female voice, catching a skinny arm in his hand. The owner snatched it away sharply, almost dragging him into the alley with her as she tried to scurry off. Beyond his confusion, he had an impression of blonde hair and called out: 'Ellen.'

The girl stopped dead and glanced back. It wasn't her. Although she was about the same age as Ellen, hardship had dulled the blueness of this girl's eyes.

'I'm sorry . . . I thought you were someone else.'

She turned fully to face him, flicking the hem of her skirt up high to reveal the length of her leg. 'I can be anyone you want me to be, cowboy, if you can pay for it.'

Slowly, Zack turned back into the street and, one shaky step at a time, headed back to the doc's. When he arrived, the house was empty and he felt a pang of disappointment. Over the past few days, he had grown accustomed to Ellen being there. She reminded him a lot of Maggie, helped him remember the good times they'd had together, reminded him why, despite McCabe's threats, he couldn't let the bounty hunter disappear without trying to make peace between them.

He wet a cloth in the pitcher next to the bed then sat down before draping it across his forehead and eyes. Maggie. It was strange. He couldn't remember his mother, but Maggie . . . he remembered everything she did, everything she said, even though their time together had been short and he had only been a small boy.

And McCabe, too, he remembered. He had been a preacher who also taught school, always practising his sermons or sitting with his nose in a book. Zack had loved to be near him as he read quietly by the fire or aloud to him and Maggie. He had wanted to be just like him. In the intervening years not a lot had changed except that books had been exchanged for guns, the hearth fire had become a campfire and dreams for the future had become revenge for the past.

A commotion outside moved into the house and Zack recognized the sheriff's bellow. Judging by the scuffle of feet and the doc's instructions, they were bringing Abe in. Reluctantly, Zack slipped off the bed, allowing the room to straighten out in front of his eyes before he retrieved his saddlebags from the corner, then headed for the door. He had been abed too long. It was time he made a move.

The doc backed into him as he made room for the men to pass carrying the makeshift stretcher. 'Are you leaving too?'

'Yep. You're going to need the room

and I don't want to be anywhere near Abe.'

'If he makes it,' the doc said, grimly.

Both men stood silent a moment. Zack tried to conjure some sympathy for his uncle, but couldn't.

'Where's Ellen?' he asked.

'She was outside the sheriff's office the last time I saw her. Isn't she here?'

'No. Where else would she go?'

The doc shook his head. 'I can't think of anywhere. She doesn't know anyone in town except for you, me and McCabe. Maybe she's with him.'

'Maybe.'

'Speaking of McCabe: I saw what happened in the street,' the doc said, speaking to Zack but craning his neck to watch the progress of the men carrying Abe. 'It doesn't concern me what it was you two were fighting about but you've had a bad concussion and another left hook like that . . . '

'I hear you, Doc, and I'm not planning on it.'

'Good.' He reached into his pocket

and pulled out a small brown bottle with a cork stopper. 'Here's a bottle of laudanum if you need it. Make sure you come back and see me in a day or two. Sooner if those headaches get worse.'

'Sure, and you can do something for me.'

Zack was about to walk away but he paused and thought, not for the first time, that he very much liked the medic who had time for everybody.

'When you see Ellen, tell her I'm staying at the hotel, will you? I'd like to see her . . . to tell her I'm not like Abe. I'm not sure she knows that.'

A clatter and a lot of cussing took the doc away without a firm promise and Zack headed out. He looked along the street to the hotel that he had seen McCabe enter earlier. Although it wasn't the only one in town he had noticed when he rode in that it looked like the cheapest and, with only a few dollars in his pocket, the best Zack could afford. He could look for a boarding house, he supposed, but the way he felt he'd be hard pressed to make it across the street, let alone trek halfway across town just to find out there were no vacancies.

He sighed hard enough to set his head aching afresh and started towards the hotel. After years of always being one frustrating step behind the bounty hunter, it seemed that now that he needed to be, he couldn't avoid him.

★   ★   ★

Josh too was thinking about the past while he rested his weary body on the lumpy hotel bed that was too short to accommodate him without causing more pain than it eased. He covered his eyes with his forearm to block out the garish striped walls, broken only by the outline of a lopsided cupboard with a door that hung precariously from one hinge.

Hell, he hadn't expected his life to amount to this. The kid was right. He had imagined himself living in a home he had built beside the church, with Maggie alongside him and a handful of kids around them. What Zack didn't know was that he and Maggie had already been to see the lawyer and that the day Abe Lawton rode into town was the day they intended to tell the boy and sign the papers that would officially make him their son.

Back then, if Josh had known, Zack's heritage wouldn't have made one bit of difference. So why did it now? After all, if it hadn't been for the kid Josh might be lying in a cold grave up on Boot Hill. It had taken guts to do what he had done: face up to Abe alone knowing he was no match with a gun or his fists. And he had saved the girl, even if he hadn't been able to save her mother.

But no amount of reasoning could change Josh's mind as he remembered clearly the day he had found Maggie raped and murdered behind the schoolhouse. And how, two days later, when he had thrown his copy of Shakespeare into her grave, he had walked to the gun shop, there to handle for the first time the Colt .45 he now wore at his hip.

Shoving the rest of it from his mind, he extinguished the lamp and pulled one of the thin blankets awkwardly about himself. Some scars were too deep. Abe Lawton. Zack Lawton. Hell, Jesus Lawton for all Josh cared. They were all cast from the same mould. Maybe the kid hadn't shown his true colours yet, but he would. And just like he had before with the rest of that outlaw breed, Josh would be there to bring him in dead or alive.

17

Ellen came awake with a groan, her eyes quickly widening against the pulsating darkness that pressed in on her. It took a moment for her to recall where she was and when she did, panic swelled in the pit of her stomach. She choked as she remembered being thrown face down on a filthy mattress in a small room, fighting with Joe as he straddled her back and lifted her skirts.

What had happened after that was too terrible to think about as she struggled to suppress the urge to vomit. Instead, she tried not to breathe in the vile odour coming from the straw mattress and filthy bedding where she lay pinned beneath the cold, dead body of Joe.

* * *

At the hotel, the old clerk with oiled hair and ruddy cheeks spun the register around and handed Zack a pen he had just dipped into the inkwell. 'I'm guessing you won't want an upstairs room so I'll put you in the room next to your friend.'

Zack noted McCabe's neat, precise signature and smiled. Apparently old habits died hard.

He added his less confident scrawl beneath it. 'Have you got anything else on the ground floor?' he asked, shoving the ledger back around.

'The only other room I've got is on the second. No offence, son, but you don't look like you could make it that far.'

Zack had been trying to forget his aches and pains, but he couldn't disagree. Just glancing at the stairs made his head reel.

'It looks worse than it is. Did McCabe have a girl with him?' he asked as Ellen once again sprang to mind. 'A little blonde with blue eyes and a pretty smile.'

'No.' The clerk turned from a row of pigeonholes on the wall behind him and handed Zack a pitted silver-coloured key with a number seven etched into it. 'Is she the reason you two had a falling-out earlier? I don't want any trouble in my place.'

'There won't be any. Which way is my room?'

The clerk sighed, apparently disappointed about something, and pointed behind Zack. 'Go along the hall and it's the third on the right. Your friend's in room five if you two need to catch up.'

After passing through the shabby lobby with its scarred floor, worn chairs and dusty chandelier, Zack paused briefly outside McCabe's door, pondering their earlier run in. It shouldn't have to end that way between them, not after all the years they had each spent waiting for the day Abe Lawton would get what was coming to him.

He raised his knuckles to knock but dropped them again. He had waited

141

sixteen years to get even with his Uncle Abe; he could be patient a couple of days to straighten things out with McCabe.

He let himself into his own room, cracking the window open to let out the musty smell that hung in the air before lighting the short wick of a lamp next to the bed. Looking around he noted that the sheets looked fairly clean and only half a dozen bullet holes dotted the walls and ceiling. Things were looking up, he decided, and when he checked the pitcher sitting on a cracked marble wash-stand he found it half-full of clean water. Pouring the contents into a matching bowl, he dunked his face into it and enjoyed the cleansing coolness while telling himself again that he could wait a few days to sort things out with McCabe.

But what about Ellen? Where had she got to?

Water dripped down his shirt as he lifted his head and groped for the towel hanging by a nail on the wall. As he patted his face dry, he wondered why he couldn't get her out of his mind. Maybe it was only because he had gotten used to having her around, looking after him. But, no, his gut was telling him different.

She was just a girl and she had been scared witless when she left the doc's house. Too scared to just disappear without at least leaving some word. Even if she didn't trust Zack, and he wouldn't blame her knowing what Abe had put her through, she trusted McCabe. But out on the street McCabe had said they should go back to the doc's house and see her so it seemed unlikely he knew where she was.

Well, he realized, McCabe wasn't going to be any help anyhow when through the thin wall between their rooms Zack could hear him already snoring. Throwing down the towel, he opened his saddle-bags, took out his gunbelt and strapped it on. Wherever Ellen was, he was going to find her and bring her back, repay some of the kindness she had shown him, make her understand he wasn't like Abe and maybe, just maybe, help her overcome the fear that had driven her away.

★ ★ ★

Ellen lay in the dark, pinned by Joe's lifeless body and paralysed by her own fear. Joe had warned her that no one knew she was there, that he could keep her a prisoner for days and no one would miss her. Was it true? Would Mr McCabe notice she was gone? Would he care now that Abe Lawton was behind bars and he could collect his bounty and leave town? And what if he did come looking and find her pinned beneath a corpse with a dagger-like shard of glass sticking in its throat, would he hand her over to the sheriff and claim a bounty on her head?

Either way, it looked like she would have to rely on herself.

Tentatively she started to move, to wriggle beneath the dead weight of a man twice her size and the reluctance of her own limbs to obey the screaming commands inside her head. But it was a painstakingly slow process, especially when every noise, from a scurrying rat to a rowdy drunk somewhere beyond the suffocating darkness, made her freeze from sheer panic.

* * *

After a cursory glance over the batwings, Zack made his way into the saloon and walked unhindered to the bar. Of the dozen or so men who were there, most were either sitting at tables playing cards or hanging on to the few girls who smiled at him despite the bruises. Besides a couple of furtive glances, nobody seemed particularly interested in him. He guessed that would be the way of it for a while until people figured out what kind of a man he was without the Lawton reputation backing him.

'Beer?'

He nodded, wishing he hadn't, and exchanged a coin for the froth filled glass the barman slid towards him. After skimming a sip off the top and wiping his lips on the back of his hand, he leaned on the bar to wait. If there was one thing he had learned during his months following McCabe, it was that if a man didn't want to draw attention by asking questions, the best place to be was within earshot of a gossipy barkeep.

Almost immediately, the barman poured a glass of whiskey and handed it to a chubby man in a derby hat and a stained grey suit who settled himself on his elbows at the bar.

'There you go, Leroy.'

The man drank it down in one. 'Thank you, Clem. Where's Joe?'

'I ain't seen him all night. He said he had some business to take care of; a new girl he needed to . . . break in.' Clem wiped the bar as he glanced in Zack's direction, his expression suddenly guarded. 'Do you need a refill on that drink, mister?'

Zack tried to relax as he shook his head, but already the implications of the barkeep's careless admission had registered. He sipped his drink, more to hide his interest than to wet the sudden dryness of his mouth.

'Hell of a shame, if you ask me,' Leroy opined, seemingly oblivious to the tension. 'I've got five dollars I owe him tucked in my pocket. I guess I'll just have to pay it back to him some other way.' Both men laughed, as if at some private joke as the man in the suit turned to survey the room and a buxom redhead sashaying between tables to meet him. 'Yep. Fifty cents for her, a dollar fifty for him and a good time for me. Everyone's a winner.'

'I wouldn't be so sure about that, Leroy. He told me he was likely to take your ear off if he didn't see that money any time soon. You know what a mean temper he's got. If you want my advice, I'd go and find him. He's probably drunk by now, sleeping it off in Clara's room.'

The buxom redhead grabbed Leroy's arm and pulled him to her bosom. 'Well while you're thinking about it, sweetheart, why don't we walk round to my place? If I can't persuade you to stay with me by the time we get there, you can walk on by and give Joe your damn money.'

Zack didn't need to hear any more. Patience had brought him the information he wanted surprisingly quickly. Now all he needed to do was make a conspicuous exit. Holding his hand to his head, he moaned loud enough to draw all their attention.

'You all right, feller?' Clem asked.

'Guess I should have taken the doc's advice and stayed in my bed a while longer.'

Leroy nodded. 'That pounding you took, you're lucky to be alive. Do you need a hand getting back?'

'No, I'll be all right. Good night.'

Zack feigned giddiness with a stagger as he pushed away from the bar, although it wasn't much of an act. The potent mix of smoke, perfume and bodily odours of all kinds that only a saloon seemed to carry, had never been to his liking and tonight his senses seemed heightened to it. He almost wished he were going back to the hotel as he turned right out of the door and melted into the shadows to wait.

★ ★ ★

With a final heave, Ellen pulled herself free and lay panting in the darkness. Now that Joe's weight was gone, her body felt ridiculously light and, as she slid to her knees on the floor, she wondered whether she could actually stand. Just as she braced herself to try, laughter alerted her to the presence of at least two people outside. Something banged against the door and she clamped her hand across her mouth, afraid that the tension inside would explode in a scream before she could stop it.

'Careful, honey,' a woman cautioned.

'I ain't averse to the kinky stuff but even I ain't prepared to do it on the bed of a dead woman.'

'That was Jenny's room?' It was a man's voice. 'Why don't we take a look? Maybe there's something valuable in there.'

The handle turned and the door opened a crack. Quickly it slammed shut.

'Leroy! Don't you think if there was, Joe would have taken it?'

'I guess so.' The man sounded disappointed but resigned.

'Then let's stop wasting time and . . . '

Even as the giggling and footsteps moved away and a door slammed nearby, Ellen couldn't bring herself to move. When that handle had turned and the door had started to open, her mind had gone off in a hundred different directions and even now she was struggling to think straight. She knew she should get out of there but this was her mother's room and she wanted to see it.

Feeling around in the dark, she found a table beside the bed and on it a lamp and some matches. With her hands still shaking, it took several seconds to strike a light and the first flash blinded her before she could put it to the wick. After a couple more attempts, she eventually set it alight, turning it so low that it spluttered, threatening to extinguish itself before she had a chance even to glimpse her surroundings.

But maybe that would have been a good thing. She couldn't even bring herself to glance at the corpse but even so the scene that greeted her was far from pleasant. No pictures adorned the wooden walls. No shelves laden with the trinkets or memorabilia that a great actress might accumulate. Nothing. Just a filthy bed, a dresser with a cracked jug and basin and a broken mirror that threw back a reflection so freakish that it repulsed and mesmerized her at the same time.

A light knock at the door snapped her back to her senses as surely as a slap in the face.

'Joe?' someone asked. 'Joe, are you in there?'

She held her breath, willing the man to leave, but instead the door eased open and he filled the doorway. Slowly, Ellen backed up, feeling Joe's dead hand touch the back of her foot. This time there was nothing she could do to stop the scream that seemed to rip her apart as she stumbled and collided with the wall behind her.

18

Zack's glance took in everything in the split second it took him to step into the room and shove the door shut. Two strides carried him over the body and across the floor and he had his hand clamped over Ellen's mouth even before he had time to consider whether he might be her next victim.

'Ellen, it's Zack. I need you to calm down and — '

Lightning-sharp pain almost split him in two as she shoved against his broken ribs. Luckily, the doc had bandaged him up tight and somehow he managed to keep his hold on her despite the violent fight she put up. Still, in his condition he wouldn't be able to hold her for long if she kept on kicking and scratching like a wildcat, and if she got loose God only knew what she might do or where she'd end up.

153

Against his better judgement he spun her around so that she faced away from him, and pinned her bodily to the wall. 'Ellen, I promise you I came here to help you.'

Virtually unable now to offer any resistance, she clung to the wall as though wishing she could disappear into it. 'Please . . . ' she pleaded. 'Please just leave me alone. Don't hurt me.'

He relaxed his hold. Ashamed. And mad. Mad at Abe. Mad at Joe. Mad at himself. He had come to find her, to tell her he wasn't like his uncle and here he was holding her against her will, up against the wall like a dollar whore.

'I'm not going to hurt you, Ellen.'

Zack eased his weight off her and stepped away completely, noticing the blood that soaked the back of her dress from neck to waist. He wanted to ask her about it but doubted he'd get an answer. From the fighting wildcat she had been a few minutes earlier, she had become completely still. He wasn't even sure she could understand him as she pleaded over and over again for him not to hurt her.

But he needed answers if he was going to help her and, awkwardly, he dropped to his knee beside the corpse and turned it over. A shard of silvered glass stuck from the side of Joe's neck and sticky blood stained his shirt over the shoulders and chest. For Zack, the corresponding blood on the back of Ellen's dress told a story he preferred not to imagine.

He closed the lifeless eyes that had stared back at him, then looked up. Ellen was facing him now, her arms wrapped around her body like a shield. Her focus was all on Joe as she mumbled almost incoherently.

'I killed him. The mirror smashed when he threw me down. I grabbed . . . ' She threw her arm wide and screwed her fingers into a fist as if gripping something, then struck up and back, again and again. 'I had to make him stop.'

Zack stood up, feeling light-headed

and slightly nauseated. The picture she painted was bad enough, but it had been a hell of a day and now the smell of blood, the oppressive stench of filth and decay and the fearful look on Ellen's face all weighed on him like a ton of rocks. Not to mention the fact that he didn't know what to do with her. The state she was in, she was likely to attack him if he made any move towards her, but he couldn't just leave her there.

'We'll go to the sheriff,' he said eventually.

Her eyes widened. 'No! Not the sheriff.'

'The evidence speaks for itself. Even that dumb old lawman will be able to see what happened. It was obviously self-defence.'

She shook her head frantically. 'He was in on it with Joe. I heard them talking.'

Zack found it hard to believe, but he wasn't always a good judge of character. McCabe seemed to be proof of that. Ellen obviously did believe it though, judging by the way she wrung her hands in the folds of her dress.

'You're hurt,' he said, noticing fresh blood appearing on her skirt.

She looked blankly at the deep gash running the width of her right palm. Then unexpectedly, she held it out towards him as though she wanted him to do something about it. For a moment, he hesitated. Losing his mother, then Maggie, at a young age had taught him a hard lesson. He had promised himself never to care about anyone, but if that was the case, he wouldn't be here now.

He clasped her wrist gently. 'Come with me.'

★   ★   ★

Doctor Morris finished cleaning the wound and took a needle and a length of fine silk thread from his bag. He handed Zack the lamp and indicated where he wanted him to hold it, near to his patient.

157

'She's right. The sheriff thinks nobody knows, but the girls over at the saloon talk to me. He's got his fingers in half the dodgy dealings in town, including selling girls to the saloon and taking a percentage of whatever they earn.'

Ellen had passed out when the doc was cleaning glass out of the wound and now Zack touched her cheek gently. She was such a pretty thing, and young. Too young to have suffered so much already. He couldn't stand by and let a corrupt lawman take away whatever chance she had for happiness.

'Do you want my advice?' the doc asked, leaning over the wound as deftly he drew the edges together with small, precise stitches.

'I'm listening.'

'Don't say anything about what happened. Make out you were never there: that she was never there. Trust me when I tell you Joe deserved what he got, however it came about.'

Zack considered the proposition but it had flaws and he was struggling to iron them out as weariness played on his injuries and dulled his senses. Several times his gaze wandered towards the medicine cabinet and the bottles of laudanum but he daren't give in to the temptation. Whatever happened, he would need all his concentration and he was already struggling with it.

Doc Morris scowled at him as the lamp wavered.

'But the barkeep, Clem, knew Joe was . . . ' Zack hesitated, abhorring the way Clem had talked about Joe's method of introducing a new girl into the business. 'He knew Joe was with a girl. I'm betting he knows it was Ellen. It won't take too much for him to put two and two together; especially given her hand's torn to bits from that glass sticking out of Joe's neck.'

They slipped into a period of silence. The only plan Zack had ever had was to find Abe and make him pay for what he'd done to Maggie and to his parents. Even then he had relied on McCabe's man-hunting skills and the slim hope that he could get the drop on Abe. That hadn't gone too well.

Doc Morris shook his head. 'There's only one thing you can do, if you want to help her. You need to get her away from here and disappear.'

'Me? She's scared to death of me.'

'McCabe then. She seems taken with him.'

It was true, but even so. 'He won't leave town until Abe's dead. He's waited too long to see it and I sure wouldn't deny him the satisfaction.'

The doc chuckled. 'It seems like you have a dilemma then. She stays here and the sheriff either decides she's innocent and life goes on, or he takes the easier option and decides she's guilty.'

'It was self-defence,' Zack countered fiercely. 'Look at the blood on her dress. He was behind her when it happened.'

The doc nodded without much conviction. 'The sheriff might look like an incompetent fool, but even in the short time I've been here I've seen more than one innocent man get on the wrong side of him and find himself on the way to the state penitentiary.' He tied off the thread and cut it with a small pair of scissors. 'Evidence can be changed. Witnesses can be found, if you know what I mean. You might even find yourself taking the blame.'

'Me?' The possibility hadn't even occurred to him.

'You're a Lawton, aren't you?'

Zack felt a familiar chill settle over him. How long would it be before that name lost its stigma? Would it ever?

'I'm not wanted for anything.'

'I know,' the doc said with some degree of sympathy, 'and I'd be the last one to judge you, but a man like the sheriff won't let a small thing like that stop him from adding your name to his bragging list.'

Zack cradled his head in his hand. The pain at his temple seemed to be throbbing at double time, obscuring the answer to his problem. His problem?

He hadn't done anything, and the girl . . . no one could blame her for what had happened. Could they? He reconsidered. If McCabe could blame him for Maggie's death, anything must be possible.

Ellen's eyelids flickered against the lamplight. 'I want to go home.'

The doc gave Zack a 'well, there's your answer' kind of a look. 'Where is home, Ellen?' he asked.

'Bluewater Creek.'

'What did you say?' Zack asked, but she was already fading away. 'What did she say?'

'Bluewater. Does that mean something to you?' the doc asked.

'Yep.' Zack felt a surge of anticipation. 'It means we're going home.'

19

'Look, McCabe, it doesn't make any difference you coming in here every day asking the same question.' The sheriff moved aside a carrot on his plate and stabbed his fork into a potato before shoving it whole into his mouth. Gravy dribbled down his chin and landed on the towel shoved inside his collar and draped over his stomach. 'I'll tell you today what I told you yesterday, last week and all the weeks before that: Judge Renwell's in bed with a busted leg and it's going to be another three weeks before he gets here. Until then, Abe Lawton — '

'Are you trying to tell me he's the only judge in the whole territory who can try this murdering bastard?'

'No, but he's the only one with a personal interest.'

Josh sighed angrily. 'We've all got a

personal interest, Sheriff. He ain't the only man who lost his wife to this scum.'

The sheriff shrugged with indifference. 'Well, as I was saying; until then, Abe Lawton will sit in that jail cell where he's been for the past five weeks. Hell, what's your problem? He'll hang sooner or later.'

Being in this town; that was Josh's problem. His wounds were about healed enough for him to ride on and the itch to get moving, to seek the solitude of wide open places, was upon him. He glanced towards the cell where Abe Lawton lay on his bed, his remaining arm wedged behind his head as he glared back at him. The verbal vitriol towards Josh had stopped a few weeks ago but hatred still burned white hot in the soulless black eyes.

Josh hoped Abe read the same loathing in his own expression.

'If you want something to do while you're waiting, why don't you go after that girl?' the sheriff offered. 'The warrant for her arrest came through over three weeks ago and I ain't seen you raise a hair. Why, she'd be the easiest three hundred dollars you ever earned, especially if you ask your friend the doc where she went. He knows more than he's letting on, if you ask me.'

Josh turned on his heel and headed out, rattling the door behind him as frustration got the better of him. Then, pausing on the plankwalk, he stopped and took a deep breath while he scanned the street. Nothing changed in the goddamn place except some of the faces. He had been right when he first arrived. It was nothing more than a stopping-off point for people with no particular destination. Why, he could have collected on a dozen dodgers in the past three weeks if he'd been of a mind to.

So, why hadn't he? For the same reason he wouldn't go after the girl? Because now he had Abe Lawton he had lost his purpose?

He shrugged his misgivings aside, telling himself it was his injuries that were stopping him, nothing else. His arm was still too stiff to draw a gun with any efficiency and his leg had a tendency to give way when he got tired. In a brawl he'd be lucky to last more than a minute with a real hardcase. Besides, he still had enough money for a few drinks and a few hands of cards.

Without looking left or right, he headed for his usual table at the saloon.

★　★　★

Three weeks later, Josh sat in his usual seat in the saloon playing cards with a drifter who had wandered into town that afternoon. Unusually, the place was quiet with only a couple of whores and a few townsmen standing around talking in hushed tones. Josh looked at the pile of winnings in front of him and decided this would be his last hand for the night; his opponent, a rough-looking older man still with trail dirt on him, was starting to look a little edgy. Besides, it was getting late and he wanted to be up early in the morning to meet Judge Renwell off the stage.

Out of the corner of his eye Josh glimpsed the batwings move and recognized Doc Morris. The medical man headed for the bar then wandered across with beer in hand to watch the game.

'How are you doing, Doc?' Josh asked, tossing another dollar into the pot.

'All right. Things are a little quiet around here. I guess all that'll change when the trial starts.' He sipped the froth from his glass. 'How are you doing, McCabe?'

Josh sensed a shift in the atmosphere but kept his focus on his cards. Maybe if he ignored the obvious it wouldn't turn into the inevitable.

But the drifter had other ideas. 'Josh McCabe! I knew I recognized you from someplace,' the stranger blurted out, seemingly unable to keep his animosity in check.

Josh slipped his hand to his gun obscured beneath the table and flicked the thong off his holster. 'I don't want any trouble,' he said without looking up from his cards.

'Well, you're sure as hell getting some.'

Josh dived to one side as the table crashed towards him, sending cards, money and drinks flying every which way. He cleared leather clumsily as he moved and fired, the action feeling stiff and laboured after the long lay-off. Glass smashed as the mirror behind the bar shattered. Luckily for him the stranger had hindered himself when he shoved the table and his first shot also went wide.

Josh rolled, coming to his knee and firing at the same time as the drifter. He felt the sting of a bullet as it crossed his scalp and saw the man stumble with blood soaking his shoulder. Josh fired again. This time crimson sprayed the room and the man went down, a patch of blood spreading at his waist testament to the fact that the bullet had found its mark.

With smoke lingering in the air, Josh kicked the fallen gun away and rolled the man over. He was still alive. He let Doc Morris get to him.

'I told you I wasn't looking for trouble, you stupid son-of-a-bitch,' Josh said. 'I don't even know you.'

The man laughed, weakly. 'The name's Will Blakeley. I'm wanted in four states for bank robbery and murder. I'd say you just earned yourself about twelve hundred dollars, give or take.'

Josh shook his head. Some men were just so stupid it made you wonder how they found their way out of bed in the morning. But, hell, if the idiot wanted a trip to jail and an audience with the judge, then Josh was happy to oblige. To be honest, the prospect of handing a man into the law and collecting the reward made Josh feel more alive than he had in a month.

'Is he all right to be moved?' Josh asked the doc.

'Yes, the bullet went through the flesh. It's not serious. I'll get my bag and meet you over at the jail.'

Grabbing Blakeley by the scruff of the neck, Josh hauled him out into the street and across to the sheriff's office. As usual, the fat old lawman was sleeping off his supper, feet up on the desk. Josh let the door bang back on its hinges as he entered.

'What the . . . ? McCabe, how many times do I have to tell you about banging that goddamn door?'

Josh shrugged. 'I brought you a prisoner. He says his name's Will Blakeley and he's wanted in four states for robbery and murder. I'll come back and collect the reward tomorrow when you've had a chance to check that.'

The lawman harrumphed as he got to his feet. 'It ain't my job to find out how much he's worth. You want the bounty you come back tomorrow morning and go through the posters.' He lumbered over to the cell next to where Abe Lawton was sleeping on his bed and opened the door. 'Bring him in here.'

Josh dragged the unconscious man into the cell and left him on the floor. 'Doc'll be over in a few minutes to clean him up. I'll be back in the morning to collect the reward.'

'Yeah, you do that,' the sheriff muttered after him. 'Sooner you get out of town the better.'

Josh ignored him, slamming the door again as he headed out and back to his hotel room for a good night's sleep.

20

The following morning, Josh stood outside the stage depot smoking a cigarette while he waited for the judge to arrive. Glancing inside the ticket office, he checked the clock above the booking clerk's desk. The overnight stage was due at 7 and already it was 7.15.

He stepped into the road to look out beyond the end of town where the sun was already climbing high in the sky. A cloud of dust lifted in the distance, so he threw down his unfinished cigarette and stepped back on the plankwalk to wait.

When the vehicle eventually rolled to a stop and the dirt settled, several passengers disembarked before the judge appeared and alighted from the dark interior. He gripped a leather satchel in one hand and a cane in the other and looked down uncertainly as he teetered on the edge of the step.

'Can I help you there, Judge?' Josh asked.

'I'd appreciate it. Damn leg stiffened up on the trip. I wouldn't like to find myself lying in the street if the damn thing gives way on me.' He chuckled. 'That wouldn't do, would it?'

Josh declined to comment, instead taking the rotund little man's arm in a firm grip. Close up, he noticed white hair beneath the felt hat and a ruddy complexion that suggested a fondness for drink. When the judge leaned into him, to roll more than to step down, Josh smelled whiskey on his breath.

'I'll get your bag.'

The judge nodded, apparently happy enough to wait and look along the street as he took a sip from a tarnished silver flask that appeared in his hand seemingly from thin air. When Josh returned with a large carpetbag, the judge generously offered him a swig.

'No thanks, Judge, I'll just take you

across to the jail, if you don't mind. I know the sheriff's been anxious to see you.'

'Not anxious enough to meet me off the stage. Unlike you, Mr McCabe.' The judge raised an eyebrow. 'That's right, I know who you are. I was hoping that one day we'd meet so I could shake the hand of the man who's single-handedly brought those murdering Lawtons to justice.'

Josh had never been comfortable with compliments and he shifted his stance, keen to make a move. 'Well, it's not all down to me. It takes men like you to pass the sentence that sees scum like them dangle from a rope. Shall we get going?'

The judge nodded decisively. 'Very true. Lead the way.'

They arrived at the jail ten minutes later, Josh having had to shorten his stride and curb his impatience to allow the limping judge to keep up. When he found the door locked, it was all he could do not to kick it in. Instead, he banged on the solid wood panels and shouted the sheriff's name. Not a sound came back to him.

'Maybe he stepped out,' the judge opined, licking his lips as his gaze wandered to the saloon opposite. 'We could come back.'

Josh shook his head. 'Even if he had, he wouldn't have left Abe Lawton alone in there.'

He shouted again through the panels. Still nothing.

'Stay here a minute while I take a look around the back.'

Despite Josh's abrupt attitude, the judge shrugged agreeably, the flask again appearing in his hand. Wondering whether the judge would be sober enough to conduct a trial, Josh moved swiftly through the alley leading to the back on the right-hand side. Not that it made a difference. The jail was detached from both its neighbours and both external side walls were solid brick, the only points of access to the small squat building being the front door and another at the rear.

When Josh rounded the corner, he could see immediately that the back door was slightly ajar and as he tiptoed closer, he slipped the thong off his gun.

'Sheriff?' he shouted, easing the door open with a fingertip so as not to show himself inside. 'Are you in there?'

A muffled, unintelligible response came back to him. Josh strained to make it out more clearly and heard the rattle of metal on metal. Without doubt, something was very wrong and Josh swallowed on a sick feeling of apprehension as he peered cautiously around the doorpost.

A glance told him that the main room was empty. The door to Abe Lawton's cell hung open and, as Josh moved further inside, he spied the sheriff lying face down on what had been Abe's cot. The lawman's own handcuffs secured him to the bars and a filthy rag had been tied around his mouth to stop him from yelling.

After taking a longer look around the

outer room to make sure no one lay in ambush, Josh marched in. His first thought was to release the sheriff, until he saw the man lying doubled up on the floor in the other cell. Ignoring the lawman's protests, he yanked against the bars, running back to fetch the keys from the outer door and fumbling as he unlocked the cell. Once inside, he dropped to his knee beside the body. There was no doubt the doc was dead. Sticky blood covered his hands where he still grasped his stomach, and the grimace of a slow, painful death was etched on his face like an ugly mask. Feeling utterly sick, Josh closed the doctor's glazed eyes and went to free the sheriff.

'What the hell happened?' he barked, yanking the gag from the lawman's mouth.

'Lawton tricked me. After the doc patched up that man you brought in, we were talking and Lawton suddenly starts shouting. He says the prisoner isn't breathing. Doc goes over to take a look then he calls me over and says he needs my opinion.' The sheriff rubbed his wrists as the cuffs fell away. His face was ashen as he sat up on the low bed. 'I was a damn fool, McCabe. I should have known the doc wouldn't need my opinion. When I bent over to listen for a breath, Lawton grabbed my gun through the bars and . . . '

Josh shook his head in disbelief. 'A one-armed man got the drop on you?'

The sheriff hung his head. 'Not exactly. It turns out the one you brought in, Blakeley, he was in on it. He had a knife on him that I didn't see. He pulled it on the doc so that he'd get me to come over, then . . . ' he shrugged as if the rest was obvious.

'And the doc? How'd he come to be gut shot?'

'Lawton did it. Said he wanted him to suffer the way he'd suffered since the doc took his arm.' The sheriff looked close to tears. 'He told me to give you a message. He said to tell you that he's going after everybody that had a part in it and then he's coming for you.'

Josh didn't doubt it.

'So why are you still alive?' he asked, weighing the injustice of the doc being dead while a fool like the sheriff still breathed.

The lawman shrugged, keeping his gaze towards the ground. 'To give you that message. He said he'd be back for me after he took care of his nephew and that girl. He said I could wait.'

The anger that had raged inside Josh when he saw the doc's body started to dwindle as his man-hunter's instincts kicked in. The whys and wherefores didn't make a difference. All that mattered was that Abe Lawton was gone and now Josh would go after him.

'How long ago did all this happen?' he asked, thinking about the state of the doc's body.

The sheriff exhaled and looked at the clock on the wall above the door. 'Last night. I'd say he's got a good twelve hours head start on you.'

'Twelve hours!'

'That's what I said.' The sheriff sounded indignant.

Josh slammed his hand against the bars. 'He could be headed in any direction. Finding his tracks now will be like finding a needle in a haystack.'

The lawman rubbed his chin thoughtfully. 'I don't know whether this will help but . . . ' He seemed reluctant to go on but Josh's impatience was tangible and the sheriff seemed to draw some fortitude from it. 'Before he died, the doc managed to say something.'

'What?' Josh asked, almost grabbing the lawman by the throat to drag the information from him.

'I couldn't hear too well, but it sounded like . . . Bluewater.'

For a second or two it seemed not to register with Josh, as though the word had come from a distance and was meant for someone else. And then the weight of it hit him and a knot of foreboding formed in the pit of his stomach. He backed away.

'Do you know what he meant?' the

sheriff asked, following as Josh turned and headed for the back door.

Josh nodded, although it was more an affirmation to himself than an answer for the lawman.

'Well?' the sheriff demanded as he followed him outside.

'It means the Devil's going back to Hell.'

21

Riding into Bluewater Creek gave Josh a jolt. He hadn't thought about the place for years and yet he remembered it being pretty much the same as he rode in along Main Street. Only as he rounded a bend in the road that had previously signified the end of town did he see the extent of Bluewater's growth.

What had been no more than a few canvas tents and some hastily erected clapboard structures had transformed into a dozen or more solidly built and well-maintained buildings offering a variety of products and services. Of particular interest was a neat café with a plate-glass window overlooking the street. His stomach had been rumbling for the past five miles and Josh was sick of jerky. He made a note to come back but continued on past a saloon with rooms to let, a hat shop called

'Mademoiselle Fifi's' and several other fine establishments selling everything from hats to horse tack.

Eventually, he reached a blacksmith and livery stable. The man working at the forge looked up and shouted a greeting before plunging a red-hot horse-shoe into a barrel of water. Then, as he wiped his hands on his pants legs, he walked round to meet Josh.

'I'm Tom Harris. Are you looking for a place to stable your horse?'

'Thinking about it.'

'Well, I charge a dollar but that includes a good rub-down and a healthy feed. On a quiet night I'll even throw in some conversation for no extra charge.' Tom laughed, letting it die with a shrug. 'How long are you in town for?'

Josh stepped down stiffly from the saddle and kicked the kinks out of his legs. 'A day or maybe two.'

'Well, it ain't a problem to me. I've got plenty of room.'

Josh peered inside the empty stable

then glanced at the corral where two horses stood watching him. 'I can see that. In fact, I noticed the town was quiet when I rode in, a few places boarded up.'

'Yep, we had a bit of trouble a couple of months back. Some folks just didn't feel right staying here after what happened. They pretty much upped sticks overnight and we're not exactly on the beaten track out here.'

Josh nodded. He knew exactly what the smith was saying. He had done the same thing years earlier; and for the same reason.

'Can you recommend anywhere good to eat?' he asked, keen to keep the man talking at his ease.

'Becky's café. You probably saw it on your way in. Looks fancy but the foods good home-cooking and the prices are reasonable. If you're looking for somewhere to stay there are rooms over the saloon. There used to be a boarding house but the lady who ran it . . . she was one of them that couldn't stay.'

Josh untied his saddlebags and pulled the carbine from its boot. 'Thanks for your help.' He started to walk away then paused and turned back as if having an afterthought. 'Maybe you could help me with one other thing?'

The smith smiled. 'I'll try.'

'I'm looking for someone; a friend. Her name's Ellen. Ellen Allbright?'

A mask dropped over Tom's expression but not before Josh read his answer. He didn't wait for the lie he knew was coming.

'Is the kid she was travelling with still in town?'

'I'll be sure to take good care of your horse, mister,' Tom assured him, turning his back and walking the animal away.

Josh shrugged and headed back towards Becky's café. Now that he thought about it, Bluewater seemed to lack the usual social graces you found in a small town. True, people could be a little cautious around strangers but they didn't usually scurry off the street when

185

he approached them.

He was almost glad of the smile the girl in the café gave him when he walked past the window and set the bell above the door chiming as he entered. However, glancing around the neat establishment with its blue-cloth-covered tables and mouthwatering aromas, he wondered whether her enthusiasm was born purely out of a need for a customer. Aside from himself, the only other client was a man who appeared to be dozing under the brim of his high-crowned hat.

Josh took a seat away from the window where he could see the street without being seen. Before he had even settled his bags at his feet, a cup and saucer were placed in front of him and a measure of thick black coffee had been poured.

'My name's Becky. The first one's on the house.' The young redhead continued to smile while she openly appraised him. 'What can I get you, stranger?'

'What's good?'

'Rabbit stew?'

'Suits me.'

The girl returned a couple of minutes later with some bread and a steaming plate. Much to Josh's amusement mixed with a mite of chagrin she took her time placing it squarely in front of him before laying out a knife and fork on either side. When she was finished, she stood back and waited, giving him an encouraging nod when he didn't immediately tuck in.

'That's good,' he said, genuinely impressed with the first bite.

'Thank you. If there's anything else you need, just give me a call.' She pointed to a table near to where a curtain separated the kitchen from the dining area. 'I'll be right over there.'

Despite his hunger, Josh took time to savour each mouthful, feeling disappointed when he swallowed the last piece of gravy-soaked bread. As he guessed she would, Becky appeared at his side almost immediately.

'I thought you might like some

apricot pie to finish off with.'

She replaced his empty plate with another. If he had been considering a refusal, the golden pastry and deep-filled centre were a mind changer. Again, Becky handed him a fork and waited for him to take a bite.

'That's the best pie I ever tasted,' he said.

Becky blushed and a thought occurred to Josh.

'Do you do all the cooking yourself?' he asked.

'Yes, sir. Ever since my ma died a couple of months back.'

Josh shoved a chair out from beneath the table: 'Do you have time to stop and talk?'

Becky looked around and shrugged. 'I guess so.'

For a few minutes they talked about her cooking, the café and how she had been running the place on her own. Then, when she was relaxed and laughing like she'd known him all her life, he said: 'You must know my niece,

Ellen. She's about your age. Ellen Allbright.'

Becky tapped her lip as she thought about it. 'The only Ellen I know is Ellen Cahill. She's about my age, I guess, or maybe a bit younger.' She chuckled. 'Old enough to leave town looking for her ma one minute and come back with a good-looking cousin she never knew she had the next.'

Josh took a minute to register the information. He remembered now that when he had first met Ellen outside the hotel she had told him her name was Cahill. Somehow, after all the commotion with Abe Lawton, people had assumed she had the same last name as her mother and he hadn't been interested enough to correct them.

'Good-looking cousin? You mean Zack,' he said, on a wild hunch.

Becky sighed. 'I do indeed.' She laughed and got to her feet, pushing the chair back underneath the table. 'And quiet. You know; the strong silent type. She's lucky to have him.

He'd do anything for her. She needs somebody like that around after what happened . . . before, you know.'

Josh nodded, able to make a pretty good guess at what Becky was alluding to. The whole town bore the scars of Abe Lawton's cruel and mindless depravity. And it all made sense, if he thought about it. Ellen's extreme fear of Abe Lawton; her unreasonable dislike of Zack. A dislike she seemed to have overcome.

'Well, I think the sooner I say hello, the better,' he said, finishing off the pie with a satisfied intake and exhalation of breath. 'Where are they at these days?'

'Out at the old MacKenzie — '

'Becky!'

The man who had appeared to be dozing was suddenly wide awake. As Becky grabbed the plates and scurried away, he straightened his hat, got up and walked over. As he drew level, Josh noticed that beneath his short coat he wore a silver star pinned to his vest. He looked up into a face that was considerably younger than he would have expected, maybe no more thirty years old, but somehow worldly wise.

'Afternoon, Sheriff,' he said, catching the hint of amusement that threatened to surface.

Although the lawman didn't recognize him, Josh knew Jimmy Hilton. He had been a gangly youth when Josh had last seen him, more interested in chasing girls and practising with a six-shooter than doing his homework.

'Afternoon. Would you like to tell me what your business is with Ellen?'

'I'm just passing through and wanted to catch up with her. Find out how she is . . . after what happened.'

The sheriff shook his head. 'Don't take me for a fool, mister. I've known Ellen since she was a baby and I know that aside from her pa, she didn't have another living relative.'

'And her ma and her cousin,' Josh reminded him.

Jimmy conceded with a slow, deliberating nod. 'Them as well, but I'm sorry, you're no missing uncle. I know a bounty hunter when I see one.' He straightened his hat again and stared out of the window while he let the knowledge sink in. 'We don't like your kind in our town and, like Becky already told you, her cousin isn't a man who's going to let you just walk in there and take her. He's likely to shoot you before you get within a hundred yards of the place. Take my advice and just ride on through.'

Josh smiled. 'I can't do that, Sheriff. I've got things I need to do. Personally, if I were you I'd be worrying about this town instead of sticking your nose into my business.'

'Is that so?' Jimmy's pale complexion flared with colour. 'Well, mister — '

'McCabe. My name's McCabe.'

The sheriff's indignation died down as quickly as it had flared up, his jaw sagging as he fixed his attention on Josh. For a second Josh thought he might put two and two together and remember the studious preacher who had so often reprimanded him for his love of guns and violence. Maybe if the face had been the same, he would have, but years spent out in the open, drinking too much whiskey, and a soul full of revenge had changed Josh on the outside as well as the inside.

Josh spoke quickly, just in case. 'Yeah, I'm the one who brought all the Lawtons to justice,' he said, before the sheriff asked. 'And on that subject, did you hear Abe Lawton escaped from jail a few days ago?'

The sheriff nodded. 'You don't think he's coming back here, do you?' He sounded worried.

'I'd bet my last dollar on it.'

'So why are you going after Ellen? She's hardly worth your trouble with that maniac in the area.'

Having the sheriff on his side might have been a help but Josh didn't feel inclined to explain his motives. 'I owe her. Why are you so dead set on protecting her, since you obviously know about the reward and why it was posted?'

The sheriff shifted uneasily. 'Ellen's no murderer and we look after our own.'

Josh shrugged and picked up his saddlebags before getting stiffly to his feet. You couldn't argue with small-town loyalty. Besides, he was in no position to judge.

'I hope you're right. Now I suggest you point me in the direction of the old McKenzie place because if you don't she won't need your protection or Zack's. She won't need anything ever again.'

22

'Rider coming!'

Zack looked up from the furrow he was ploughing, first towards the winding road leading from the distant foothills and then to Ellie who stood on the porch, shading her eyes from the mid-afternoon sun as she too watched the approaching rider. Whoever the man was, he seemed in no hurry as his horse walked towards the small homestead.

'Ellie, go inside the house until I find out what he wants.'

She didn't hesitate and he smiled despite the anxiety building inside him. It had taken a long time to build her trust and even now it was a fragile thing. Visitors still worried her, and in turn worried him. He vaulted the fence with ease and ducked inside the house to pick up his rifle, pausing a moment to give Ellie a reassuring wink.

When Zack emerged into the sunlight, the rider was coming around the corral. He sat easy in the saddle, his hands resting loosely on his thighs. Zack couldn't get a good look at him because his face was shadowed by the wide brim of his sweat-stained felt hat.

'Howdy. You must be Zack Lawton,' the stranger called out. 'My name's William Blakeley and I'm guessing that pretty little thing in the house must be Ellen.'

A hard lump of apprehension formed in the pit of Zack's stomach and he had to swallow several times before he could get any words out. 'Stop right there.' He raised the rifle. 'I don't want to kill you, but if you've come looking for trouble you won't be disappointed, bounty hunter.'

★　★　★

Josh had spent a long time studying the homestead since it came into sight and as he got closer the features slipped into place. Smoke lifted from the chimney of a small stone built house with a narrow porch running across the front and a patch of new shingle on the roof. Chickens pecked dirt in the front yard, which was enclosed by a little picket fence in need of some repair and a coat of paint. Beyond that he noted a solid-looking barn and a small corral where a couple of horses stood three legged in the sunshine.

The narrow winding road he was heading along cut between the house and a field where he could make out a man ploughing with a big beige-coloured horse. He saw a woman come from the house and heard her voice on the breeze without knowing what she said. It was pretty easy to guess though when she disappeared back inside and the man jumped the fence and followed her.

It was what Josh would have expected; nothing out of the ordinary.

By the time he reached the end of the

house, the man in the denim coloured pants and faded shirt was waiting for him in the doorway. Josh registered the hostility etched on the sun bronzed face, and reined up keeping his hands shy of the gun at his hip and the rifle in its saddle boot. Just because the kid didn't appear to have a gun, didn't mean the girl in the house didn't have a bead on him.

'Easy, kid, I just came to talk.'

Zack raised an eyebrow.

'I came to tell you Abe busted out of jail. He murdered the doc and told the sheriff he was coming after you two then me. I know you don't care what happens to me, but the fact you're here working a homestead with the girl proves you care what happens to her.'

'Yeah, we heard.' Zack said.

Josh saw Zack's Adam's apple bob a couple of times, saw his gaze wander back towards the house.

'I didn't think you'd show up here though. You and I didn't exactly part company on friendly terms. As I recall, you threatened to shoot me on sight.'

Josh frowned. Being back in Bluewater had opened up a lot of old wounds. And now here he was, facing yet another. Except that he had visited Maggie's grave and seen that it was well-tended with fresh flowers against the headstone. Someone had told him that the young feller out at the old McKenzie place came in every week to see to it. Against all his bone-headed stubbornness, that single act had gone some way towards mellowing him until he came face to face with the kid's unforgiving attitude.

'Ellen!' Josh called, deciding she might see reason more easily than Zack. 'It's Josh McCabe. Don't be afraid; I don't mean you any harm. I'm going to step down and come in so we can talk, that's all.'

Awkwardly, Josh swung his leg out of the stirrup and over.

'No!'

Ellen's shriek confirmed Josh's uneasiness a split second too late as Abe Lawton appeared in the doorway. His nemesis fired off a couple of hurried shots as he kicked Zack into the yard before backing inside and slamming the door. In the same instant, Josh yanked the rifle from its boot as he slid to the ground, dropping behind his horse's flank and dodging frightened chickens as he tried to assess the situation.

A window shattered and a bullet whistled past Josh's ear. He saw Zack mount the porch but a couple more quick shots from inside the house drove him back and he grabbed his arm as it spurted blood. A bullet nicked Josh's horse. The animal reared, snatching the reins out of his hand and leaving him exposed when it bolted. Another bullet kicked up dirt at Josh's feet, too close for comfort, and he lunged for the kid, the action carrying them both on into the stables.

Ellen's screams mingled with the sound of a few more gunshots that hit the barn, splintering wood. And then it was over; at least on the outside.

'I ought to kill you right now, McCabe! How the hell did you let Abe slip through your fingers again? His neck was practically in the noose when we left,' Zack shouted.

He picked himself up from the floor, breathing heavily and swaying slightly as he clasped his arm. Blood ran through his fingers and disappeared inside his cuff.

'I'd save it until we get out of here; if we get out of here. It sounded to me like there was another shooter.' Josh peered out of the door, careful to keep out of sight. 'That means Abe found himself a partner. Am I right?'

Behind him he heard movement and turned, expecting trouble. Instead he saw Zack walk calmly to a long box half-buried under a pile of old blankets and straw. He yanked it open exposing a small arsenal that included a couple of old rifles, a shotgun, two handguns and several assorted boxes of ammunition. Although not new, everything looked to be in clean working order.

Zack pulled out a belt with a .45 tucked in the holster.

'It looks like you've been expecting trouble,' Josh commented as he peered over Zack's shoulder.

'Even out here we get bounty hunters,' Zack said, sounding surprisingly calm for a man with a bullet in his arm and God only knew what madcap plan running through his head. 'And make no mistake; I'll kill any man who means to harm Ellie.'

Josh didn't doubt it. He yanked his shirt out of his trousers and tore a strip off the bottom. 'Well, you better let me take a look-see at that arm or you won't be helping anyone.'

Zack looked at the blood soaking his sleeve as though he'd forgotten about it. After a second, he sat down heavily in the dirt and unbuttoned his shirt, peeling it away from the wound before looking away. Josh couldn't hide his smile, although he was glad the kid didn't see it.

'So how did they get the drop on you?'

'Blakeley rode up to the front of the house.' Zack winced. 'I thought he was a bounty hunter and while I was dealing with him Abe sneaked in the back way.'

'Blakeley?'

'That's what he called himself. Do you know him?'

Josh nodded. 'I put a slug in him but not deep enough, it seems. He was the one who broke Abe out of jail.' He shoved his regret aside and went back to examining Zack's gunshot wound. 'It looks like a through and through. All we can do for now is bind it and try to stop the bleeding.' He grabbed Zack's hand and slapped it on his head. 'Keep it there for a couple of minutes.'

Zack started to argue but Josh was already heading back to the door. After a couple of minutes of staring towards the house, he started a tour of the barn. It was a basic, small affair, big enough for two horses at most. The only way in or out was by the front unless you kicked your way out, which wouldn't help since the area between the barn and the house was in plain sight of the windows. He returned to where Zack was slumped against the wall and started to wrap his wound.

'Did you see anything?' Zack asked sounding a little breathless.

'No. It seems as though they're waiting for us to make the first move, which is damn inconvenient since they've got a clear line of sight on us as soon as we move outside this barn.' He tied off the makeshift bandage. 'Damn, I wish I'd had time to look around before they got here. You know the place, tell me about the layout.'

'It's what you saw.'

'What about the house?' Josh asked.

'There's a door at the front and another at the back, but Abe had Blakeley barricade that one. It'd take too long to bust in by which time we'd be drilled with lead and Ellie would be dead.' Zack sighed. 'There's only one thing we can do.'

'What?' The answer was slow in

coming and Josh's patience was becoming strained. He hated not being in control but with Abe holding the best vantage point, that was exactly the position he found himself in. 'If you've got a plan, kid, I'm all ears.'

Zack frowned. 'I might have, but before we partner up, I want your word on something.'

Josh waited, although he could guess what it was.

'When this is over, you leave Ellie and me alone. You get Abe Lawton for the price of the two of us.'

'Only Ellen has a price on her head,' Josh corrected him, 'but I hear you.' He nodded and held out his hand. 'You always did have me figured all wrong, kid.'

Zack shook on it, a trifle reluctantly, Josh thought. Good. The kid was learning not to be so trusting at last.

'We play to his weakness.'

Josh didn't quite understand, although suspicion prickled at the back of his neck.

'He likes to look in a man's eyes and see him suffer when he kills him.' Zack let the idea hang. 'He knows we're all in this together, that's why he didn't kill me and Ellie. He waited for you to get here; three for the price of one.'

It made sense; sense for a twisted son-of-a-bitch like Abe Lawton.

'So what are you saying: we call him out?' Josh shook his head. 'Just because he only has one arm doesn't make him any less dangerous.' He didn't want to admit he wasn't sure he was fast enough to take the gunman down. 'Besides, Blakeley's in there and he owes me one for that bullet hole he's carrying in his side.'

'Maybe so, but he's taking orders from Abe now, and if you were working with Abe, would you go against anything he told you to do or not to do?'

The kid was making sense, but there were a lot of ifs and maybes and they stayed Josh's tongue despite his burning desire to get in there and finish it.

'Have you got a better idea?' Zack asked after a few seconds.

He didn't have. 'Just promise me one thing, kid. If he takes me down, you'll bury me next to Maggie.'

23

Despite the thundering beat of her heart, Ellen sat passively at the kitchen table where Abe had pushed her after he dragged her inside. Even as Blakeley kicked over chairs, yanked open dresser drawers and sent blue-and-white crockery and a stack of books sailing across the room with a slash of his hand, she remained unmoved. When there was nothing left to break, Abe's deranged sidekick closed in on Ellen and yanked her up by the arm.

'Do you want me to make her scream, Abe? Give 'em a reason to storm the place so you can pick 'em off?' He squeezed her breast.

She twisted in his grip and spat in his face. 'If that's the best you can do, I wouldn't give you the satisfaction.'

Abe left his spot by the window and circled the table. 'Huh, look who's all grown up now. What about me? Would you still scream for me?'

She knew she would but she'd be damned if she was going to admit it.

'A one-armed man?' She laughed, hoping it sounded mocking. 'You don't frighten me any more, Mr Lawton.'

Abe gripped her chin between his fingers, digging the nails into her flesh as he looked hard into her eyes. She didn't flinch, although it took all her courage not to fold with her insides quivering fit to dissolve. Abe had always frightened her with his dark soulless stare but whereas there had been a hint of manic humour in it before, there was nothing but hatred behind it now.

'That's quite a glare you've got going on there, girly. I heard you'd killed a man, but I didn't believe it until now,' he said.

'I almost killed you twice, didn't I?' she said, hoping to unsettle him, even in some small way, and give Zack a chance.

Abe's knuckles smashed against her

cheek, the force driving her into Blakeley who staggered enough to put her out of reach of Abe's next assault. Abe himself wobbled as he over-stretched. Without his right arm, he had to twist and take the weight on his left hand to stop himself falling. His face was flushed with anger when he righted himself and raised his hand again.

Ellen closed her eyes but instead of the blow she expected, she heard a ripping, popping sound and felt the front of her dress part as buttons flew across the room. She tried to cover her half exposed breasts but Blakeley held her arms as he laughed against her ear.

'Hobble her and tie her wrists,' Abe said, stalking to the window and twitching the edge of the curtain. 'And remember what I told you, Blakeley. Zack and McCabe are mine. When they're dead, you can do what you like with the girl, but you get between me and them and I'll shoot you dead, do you understand?'

Josh took a deep breath and gave Zack a reassuring nod. The kid had lost most of his colour and already fresh blood seeped through his shirtsleeve.

'Are you sure about this?' Josh asked, shoving a spare .45 into the back of his pants and straightening his coat over the top. 'Once we're out in the open — '

'I know the risks, McCabe, but what else can we do?' Zack snapped. 'He's got Ellie. The longer we sit around on our backsides the more chance she'll get hurt. I promised her, McCabe . . . I promised I'd never let anyone hurt her again. I've made enough promises I couldn't keep. I won't add this one to the list, so either back my play or keep out of my way.'

He looked Zack in the eye. Pain, anger, fear and frustration contorted the kid's features into a mask of near insanity. Josh knew there would be no reasoning with him. If he had had the same chance to save Maggie, Josh knew he would have taken it without blinking an eye.

'I guess since this is where it all started, it's poetic justice that this is where it should end,' he said stepping aside so that Zack could take a position by the door. He chuckled despite the tension in the air. 'When this is over, we'll either be joining the ghosts of Bluewater Creek or laying them to rest.'

Zack stared at him for a long moment then smiled. 'I didn't know you had a soul, McCabe.'

Josh shrugged and the brief reverie ended as quickly as it had begun. They both looked towards the house. Apart from a broken window, the place appeared peaceful enough. There had been some noise a few minutes before that sounded like crockery breaking, but now there was only silence inside.

'Abe. Uncle Abe,' Zack shouted. 'Let Ellie go. This is between you, me and McCabe so let's all step out in the open and finish it like men.'

Unexpectedly, the door of the house opened and Ellen shuffled into view. Her head was down, her long hair hanging in front of her like a golden veil. Blakeley slipped out behind her and grabbed a fistful, yanking her head up and back to reveal her half nakedness and the red welt on her cheek. With a leer, he wrapped his arm around her, keeping the pistol in his other hand pointed at her head, and dragged her across the porch to lean against the rail.

Josh saw Zack stiffen and understood his anger but he put a restraining hand on his shoulder. 'Easy, kid. That's what he wants. You get mad, you make a mistake. Just wait.'

Within seconds Abe appeared in the doorway. Strangely, he still wore two tied-down guns despite the loss of his right arm, which was obvious to anyone by the sewn-up sleeve of his shirt. Josh lifted the rifle from the floor beside him and started to take aim.

Zack swiped at the barrel. 'Take your

own advice, McCabe, and wait. He might be a one-armed man but he still has the advantage while Blakeley's holding Ellie.'

The kid was right but it didn't make the opportunity of taking Abe without a one-on-one showdown any less tempting. Reluctantly, he surrendered the idea. Life had been a lot less complicated when the only person he had to think about was himself.

'There she is, boy,' Abe called across the yard. 'I held up my end of the bargain, now you and McCabe hold up yours and show yourselves.'

★   ★   ★

Ellen told herself over and over again to stay calm as first Zack and then McCabe stepped out into the yard, hands covering their holstered guns. But it was a hard task, seeing Zack with blood soaking his shirt-sleeve, no colour in his face and a sway in his step. Only the worry that she might distract them

214

and give Abe a split second of unguarded opportunity stopped her hysteria exploding in a fit of kicking and screaming, although Abe swaggering out to meet them with all the confidence of a prize rooster nearly tipped her over the edge. She didn't need to see his face to know he'd be smiling.

'That's close enough,' he said when they were no more than twenty feet apart. 'Let's not waste time. Which one of you dead men wants to go to Hell first?'

'What makes you think we won't both draw on you at the same time?' Josh asked.

Abe chuckled. 'Honour? Stupidity? My ace in the hole?'

Ellen believed the truth of what Abe was saying; at least where Zack was concerned. She had come to know him well in the past weeks and although he bore the Lawton name, he was no unscrupulous killer. But McCabe? He was a man used to dealing out death.

He knew the risks in letting an opponent have an even chance. Even now she could see him weighing up the odds as he looked narrowed-eyed between her and Abe.

24

Zack was scared; more scared than he had ever been in his life. He wondered whether the weakness in his legs was from loss of blood or pure fear. Either way, he could feel himself swaying and longed to shift his stance, but with Abe's merciless glare boring into him, he daren't move.

There was no mercy in Abe's dark eyes. Abe wanted to kill him and Zack didn't want to die.

'I can see you get the picture, McCabe,' Abe said, 'But I'll spell it out anyway. I've only got one gun arm.' He indicated his stump with a quick dip of his chin as though they wouldn't have noticed. 'That could make this an unfair fight. So, to make it fair,' he laughed, 'fairer for you, I'm going to take you on one at a time. That's where the girl comes in.'

'Leave her out of this,' Zack snapped, feeling useless as he glanced in Ellen's direction.

'I can't do that. She's my insurance. If you both try to draw on me at the same time, she dies and all bets are off. You got that, Blakeley?' He spoke to his partner without even bothering to look in his direction.

'Sure, boss.'

Zack tensed. The face of his mother, a long-forgotten image, flashed before his eyes and he remembered how she had suffered before she died. How Abe had left her bleeding to death with a bullet in her stomach. And he remembered Maggie. Kind, beautiful Maggie. Her death had been no less horrific after Abe had finished with her.

Zack tensed and his hand moved closer to his gun despite his best efforts not to make a stupid move. Abe's eyes crinkled at the corners as a quiver of amusement twitched his mouth, but he didn't even flinch.

Zack's senses shrieked until he

wondered whether the sound was coming from his lips. Or maybe it was Ellie screaming. He wouldn't blame her, after everything she'd been through before with Abe, and then with Joe. It was a wonder she hadn't lost her sanity before this.

He glanced in her direction, unable to look into the hate-filled eyes of his uncle any longer. Maybe it was his imagination, but he thought she smiled at him. Then Blakeley whispered something against her ear and her expression changed as the outlaw released his grip on her waist, grabbed what was left of her dress and yanked.

As it was probably intended to do, the sound of cloth tearing shattered the uneasy stand-off. Everyone moved at once. Zack grabbed for his gun and heard the boom of a shot but he felt nothing as he lunged for the porch. He saw Ellie crash into the dirt, thrown away like a rag doll as Blakeley swung the pistol in his direction. They both fired. Zack felt the burn of a bullet against his thigh as he crashed to the ground, the gun skittering several feet away from him as he lost his grip on it. But it didn't matter. Blakeley was already lying face down on the porch, unmoving.

Zack held his breath, stunned by the realization that he had killed a man. In the sun drenched yard, nothing stirred. He had been aware of other shots, of movement around him, but the chaos that had erupted had ceased as quickly as it started. Only the buzzing in his ears and the acrid stench of gunpowder remained of a fight that had been looming for more than fifteen years and had lasted less than a minute.

'Ellie?' he whispered.

She lay face down in the dirt and as he tried to crawl towards her he noticed blood in her hair.

'Ellie!'

A bullet hit the ground ahead of him before he could move and he rolled on to his back, his heart sinking. McCabe lay motionless, flat out in the dirt.

Blood trickled down his temple and pooled in the dust at his shoulder. It was impossible to know whether he was alive or dead.

Abe stood over him, grinning. 'It was always gonna end like this,' he said. 'I can't die. The Devil locked his gates to me a long time ago.'

He turned fully to his nephew and Zack felt a chill tremble through him as he stared death in the face.

'It's over,' Zack said, unable to tear his gaze away from the blood soaking Abe's shirt. 'You're through. You just don't know to fall over yet.'

Abe shuffled towards him, the gun wobbling in his hand as he took aim. 'Didn't you hear what I said? I can't die. There ain't a place special enough for me in Hell.' His voice sounded hollow but his laugh was as maniacal as ever. 'But you can say hello to McCabe and that girl for me when you get there.'

Abe pulled the hammer back on his .45 and Zack closed his eyes. He didn't want the last face he saw to be that of his uncle. Instead he pictured Ellie the way she looked when he made her laugh. He was glad he had been able to bring some happiness back into her life, the way she had brought it into his.

Abe grunted. 'You again. Jesus, you're more stubborn than I am.'

Zack opened his eyes but before he knew what was happening two shots exploded so close together it was hard to tell them apart. Abe staggered, dropped to his knees and keeled over. He twitched for a second or two and then lay still.

Zack's gaze shifted to McCabe but he hadn't moved. Coming to his elbow, Zack stared around, his gaze reaching at last to a point behind him. Ellie's face showed complete surprise as she stood staring at him, the smoking gun still clutched between her hands.

'God, no. Please, not Ellie,' Zack whispered, seeing only the mass of blood staining her dress.

She dropped the weapon and started

towards him but then the pain and the realization seemed to hit her. By the time Zack reached her, she was already lost to him.

★ ★ ★

Three weeks later

Zack took a deep breath, straightened his collar and loosened his vicelike grip on the bunch of flowers he was holding. The sun was still rising in the morning sky but it was already shaping up to be a warm day. A gentle breeze bent the grass as he limped between crude wooden crosses and craftsman-shaped-and-chiselled headstones. Each one told a story but he paid no mind to them today.

Stopping in a secluded corner, shaded by a great, leafy oak he dropped his chin respectfully to his chest and quietly recited a few words from Psalm 24: 'Who shall ascend the hill of the Lord? And who shall stand in his holy place? He who has clean hands and a pure heart, who does not lift up his soul to what is false and does not swear deceitfully. He will receive blessing from the Lord and righteousness from the God of his salvation.'

He dropped to his knee, picked up a few fallen leaves and scattered them more ferociously than he intended. Sadness still filled his heart but the pain had grown less since Abe's body had been buried in an unmarked grave. He gathered up a withered bunch of flowers and set them aside.

'I picked these from the meadow behind the house,' he said, carefully placing the fresh blooms across the grassy mound. 'You always loved flowers around you.'

A hand touched him on the shoulder but he didn't need to look up to know it was the preacher.

'You need to let her go, kid.'

'I know, McCabe, but she meant a lot to me, even in the short time we had together.'

Zack sighed and got awkwardly to his

feet. He couldn't help glancing at the dark suit and shirt contrasting with the white collar. It was hard to believe this was the same man who had killed men for money, but then again, it was hard to believe that the man hunter had ever been a mild-mannered preacher.

'I know,' McCabe said. 'I feel the same way, but she's at rest now and you've got your whole life left to live. Besides . . . ' He lifted his hand and waved to a woman walking towards them, silhouetted against the sun. 'She still needs you. And she loves you.'

Ellie ran the last few yards into Zack's embrace and he felt a sense of peace replace the gloominess that had settled over him. As they all walked together down towards the church, they each knew the past would haunt them from time to time, but at least the ghosts of Bluewater Creek had been laid to rest.

We do hope that you have enjoyed reading this large print book.

Did you know that all of our titles are available for purchase?

We publish a wide range of high quality large print books including:
Romances, Mysteries, Classics General Fiction Non Fiction and Westerns

Special interest titles available in large print are:
The Little Oxford Dictionary Music Book, Song Book Hymn Book, Service Book

Also available from us courtesy of Oxford University Press:
Young Readers' Dictionary (large print edition) Young Readers' Thesaurus (large print edition)

For further information or a free brochure, please contact us at:
**Ulverscroft Large Print Books Ltd., The Green, Bradgate Road, Anstey, Leicester, LE7 7FU, England.
Tel:** (00 44) 0116 236 4325
Fax: (00 44) 0116 234 0205